THE HAUNTED INN

A LIN COFFIN COZY MYSTERY BOOK 8

J. A. WHITING

To hear about new books and book sales, please sign up for my mailing list at:

www.jawhitingbooks.com

❀ Created with Vellum

For my family with love

1

Carolin Coffin and her cousin, Viv, were completing a two-hour walk along the bike paths and streets of Nantucket and had come into the historic town from the Cliff area of the island. Weaving up and down the historic cobblestone roads, they headed along Centre Street and then the two turned right onto Gaylord Street.

Perspiration showed on Viv's forehead and some strands of her light golden brown hair stuck to the skin. "I don't know how I let you talk me into this walk. Let's take the direct way back to your house or you're going to have to carry me the rest of the way. Enough is enough. I'm beat." Viv preferred to keep athletic pursuits to a minimum, but her cousin was always suggesting a walk or a bike ride around the island.

Lin chuckled. "I'm not sure I can carry you. I'll have to call a cab to come and get you."

The early September afternoon was hot and slightly humid. The trees' leaves hadn't yet begun to turn from greens to reds, oranges, and yellows, but here and there, the edges of some bushes had already turned to scarlet.

"When is it going to cool off?" Viv fussed. "It's September, for Pete's sake."

Lin removed the Nantucket-red baseball-style hat she'd purchased at the shipwreck museum, ran her hand over the top of her sweaty head, and slipped the hat over her long brown hair. "Maybe we can go for a swim after work tomorrow afternoon. We should enjoy the last warm days of summer."

"That sounds good to me." Viv owned a popular bookstore and café on Main Street. "I'll see how busy the day is. I think I can get away for an hour or two. Don't forget we're having dinner on John's boat tomorrow night." Viv had been dating John, a successful Nantucket Realtor, for eight years, and they both played together in a band a couple of nights a week. John had lived on his boat down at the docks for nearly five years and he, Viv, Lin, and her boyfriend, Jeff, enjoyed getting together and relaxing on the boat or taking day trips around Nantucket Sound on the weekends.

The thirty-year-old cousins admired the front gardens of the homes they passed. Lin, a landscaper, pointed out the different flowers in some of the window boxes.

As they approached the Seaborne Inn, a chill ran over Lin's arms and she absent-mindedly rubbed at the goosebumps.

Viv eyed her. "Are you cold?"

"I'm feeling chilly. It's because I'm sweaty and a breeze came in off the water."

"Really?" Viv pushed a lock of hair out of her blue eyes. "I didn't feel a breeze. You don't see anyone, do you?"

Lin shook her head. "Just because I feel cold doesn't mean someone is about to make an appearance."

"Well, it usually does," Viv said softly, looking around the front yards and to the porches of the houses they passed by.

Lin had a special ability that had been passed down to her through generations of her Nantucket ancestors ... she could see ghosts.

Passing the inn, Lin's inner core became icy cold and as her eyes darted around looking to see if someone was about to show up, she worried that her cousin's suspicion might be correct.

"I'd like to stay in that inn sometime," Viv said. "There are beautiful gardens in the back. Maybe one of these days, I'll talk John into a romantic overnight."

Lin didn't comment because she was chilled to the bone and was trying to figure out why.

"You know the inn used to be a silk factory in the 1800s?" Viv asked. Built in 1835, the inn was a gray-shingled building with white trim that had once housed the Island Silk Company. The business closed after about nine years, and the factory was divided into two separate dwellings. Since 1870, one side was used as a boarding house and inns of various names. It had been the Seaborne Inn for the last twenty-five years.

"Huh?" Lin asked. "What did you say?"

Viv gave her cousin a wary look. "What's wrong with you?"

"Nothing," Lin fibbed. "I was checking out the landscaping."

"What else are you looking at?" Despite having lived on Nantucket most of her life and having some of the same ancestors as Lin, Viv couldn't see ghosts, but she usually knew when one appeared because of the way Lin behaved.

"There isn't anything," Lin said. "I'm really cold, but I don't see anything."

"That doesn't mean someone isn't lurking," Viv muttered and slipped her arm through her cousin's in order to quickly propel her up to the corner of the next street where they turned left.

Lin's chill lessened the further away from Gaylord Street they moved until she was back to normal temperature by the time they passed the Maria Mitchell Association building, a non-profit organization created to preserve the legacy of the country's first woman astronomer.

"I feel better," Lin said. "It must have been the breeze."

Viv tilted her head. "Except I was walking right beside you and I didn't feel any breeze at all."

When the cousins reached Lin's pretty, gray-shingled cottage located across from the Quaker cemetery, they headed for the kitchen for a cold drink. Lin's small brown dog, Nicky, and Viv's regal gray cat, Queenie, had been snoozing out on the deck and when they heard the young women returning from the walk, Nicky darted into the house through the doggie door to welcome them. Taking her time,

Queenie rose, stretched, and then meandered inside to greet Viv and Lin.

Viv went to the large, wooden, kitchen hutch for two tall glasses while her cousin removed pitchers of iced tea and lemonade from the refrigerator. She took a glance at the two sailor's valentines perched on the shelf of the hutch.

"The valentines look really nice together." Viv carried the glasses to the refrigerator and used tongs to place ice cubes in each of them.

As Lin poured the tea over the ice, she smiled and glanced at the valentines. "I like them in the kitchen so I can see them when I'm working in here."

Sailor's valentines were a kind of shellcraft made of tiny sea shells. The designs were placed in octagonal wooden boxes with glass fronts that displayed the shells of different colors laid out in intricate, symmetrical patterns. Common designs included compass roses, hearts, flowers, an anchor, or other sea-related objects. The early valentines were made in the 1800s, many on the island of Barbados where sailors would purchase the beautiful shellwork for a family member or loved-one.

Not long ago, Lin had bought one of the valentines from a store in Nantucket town. The tiny pinkish, cream, white, and purple shells formed a repeating design of small and large flowers surrounding a cameo set in the middle of the box ringed by pink and white shells.

The second valentine had been given to Lin for her thirtieth birthday by her landscaping partner and friend, Leonard. The valentine had once belonged to Leonard's wife, Marguerite, who had passed away in a car accident. It showed a heart in the center of a compass rose created with tiny pink, pale blue, and white shells that spread out to the edges of the box in a pattern of small flowers. The words, *Remember Me*, had been formed in an arc over the compass rose.

Lin put the glasses and some cheese and crackers on a tray and they headed for the deck to sit at the wooden table.

"I'm glad that last case is over and done with and I don't have to be afraid of that valentine anymore," Viv said holding the door to the deck open so that Lin could go outside.

A ghost from the most recent case Lin had helped with had used one of the valentines to give the young woman clues that led to the solving of the mystery.

"Yeah, I'm glad that mystery is over, although I

was never afraid of the valentine." Lin placed the tray on the table and sat down.

Viv raised an eyebrow in disbelief. "Oh, yes, you were."

Nicky let out a little woof of agreement and Lin laughed. "Okay, maybe I was a little afraid. Sometimes."

Recalling the details of that case caused a coil of anxiety to settle in Lin's stomach. She tried to push the thoughts from her mind by thinking about the walk they'd just returned from and focused on the beautiful sights they'd passed ... the green fields, the white sand beaches, and the historical homes, both grand and quaint.

Lin reached for a piece of cheese from the platter and chewed it slowly while listening to her cousin talk about the bookstore and a new gig she and John and their band had coming up.

"You and Jeff should come to hear us. We've added new songs to the playlist."

"As long as you don't call me up to the stage to sing with you." Lin gave her cousin the evil eye.

"I promised I would never do that again." A wide smile formed over Viv's mouth remembering the time she'd invited a terrified Lin up to the stage. "If only to keep you from killing me over it."

A flash of adrenaline raced through Lin's body when her cousin said the word, *killing*, and she could feel the blood drain out of her head. An involuntary shiver made Lin's body shudder.

Viv saw the change that had come over Lin. "Are you cold, again?"

"Yes." Lin could barely push the word from her mouth, her body had begun shaking so badly. With trembling fingers, she reached up and held her white-gold, antique horseshoe necklace between her thumb and forefinger. The necklace had been owned by an ancestor and was found in a storage room of Viv's Cape house, hidden there in the eighteenth-century by Sebastian Coffin, her relative and an early settler of Nantucket.

Nicky jumped up and stared across the deck to the wooded area behind the house. His little tail swished back and forth.

Lin followed the dog's gaze and she startled when she saw the figure at the edge of the trees.

The ghost of her ancestor, Sebastian Coffin, dressed in his eighteenth-century clothing, stood in the tall grass, his eyes pinned on the freezing young woman shaking in her seat at the table.

"Lin?" Viv asked, her tone tinged with worry. "Is someone here?"

"Yes." The word floated on the air. "Sebastian is here."

As soon as Lin said the words, the cottage's front doorbell rang and the atoms of Sebastian's translucent form shimmered with light and slowly disappeared.

2

Lin was still clutching her necklace and her eyes were glued to the spot where Sebastian had been standing. She hadn't seen her ancestor for weeks, and now, his appearance combined with how nervous and uneasy she'd felt as she and Viv walked up Gaylord Street earlier, spelled one thing ... trouble.

"Is Sebastian still visible?" Viv asked.

"He's gone." Lin looked out to the grassy place where Sebastian had shown up.

"The doorbell rang a second ago. I'll go see who it is." Viv got up from her seat at the table.

"Someone rang?" Lin shook herself and watched Viv open the screen door to the living room.

Nicky had already darted inside to the front of the house.

After taking a long drink of her iced tea, Lin blew out a breath and with her mind flooding with questions about Sebastian's appearance, she forced herself to her feet and headed to see who had pressed the doorbell. Before taking three steps, she heard Libby Hartnett's voice.

Libby, a lifelong resident of the island, was a trim, fit, older woman whose age the cousins were unsure of. Lin and Viv guessed that she might be in her early seventies. Libby was Lin's distant cousin and the woman had powers of her own. Since Lin had returned to Nantucket from the mainland to make her home in the cottage she'd inherited from her grandfather, Libby had been an invaluable help ... assisting Lin in her understanding and use of her "skills".

Libby rarely made a visit to the cottage, so when Lin heard the voice, it sent cold concern rushing through her veins.

The silver-haired woman burst through the door and stepped onto the deck.

"Carolin," Libby said with a serious expression. "I apologize for barging in like this, but there's a situation."

Lin's throat tightened. "A situation?"

Libby moved closer. "There's a dead body a few streets away from here."

"A dead body?" Viv nearly shrieked as she came out of the house. "Who is it? Where is it?" Looking over both of her shoulders, Viv moved close to Lin's side and wrapped her arms around herself.

Libby ignored Viv's outburst. "It's a woman. In her late thirties or early forties. Anton and I knew her casually. She was planning to stay on the island for about a month."

"Are the police investigating?" Lin asked with a hopeful tone.

"I'd like you to come with me." Libby touched her young cousin's arm. "Please. We need to go."

"Why do you want Lin to go with you?" Viv asked the question her cousin had been thinking, but didn't want to come right out with. "Where are you going?"

Libby flashed Viv a look of annoyance. "We really need to hurry. We can walk there. Over to Academy Hill."

Lin's heart dropped into her stomach. "Academy Hill?"

"Come on. I'll explain as we walk." With brisk efficiency, Libby wheeled for the door.

Hurrying over the neighborhood streets, Libby

told the young women what she knew. "The body is in a garden behind a house on Gaylord Street."

Viv looked at her cousin. Now they knew why Lin had felt so cold walking along that lane not long ago.

"Is the body at the inn?" Lin asked.

"No. Maura Wells was staying at the inn, but she was found two houses down from there. The owner of the house saw Maura sitting in one of the outdoor chairs in her backyard. The owner was very irritated that someone had trespassed and wandered into her garden. She went outside to have words with the trespasser and when she got close, she was horrified to find out the woman was dead."

"Were there visible injuries?" Viv questioned.

"None," Libby replied.

"Then Ms. Wells must have died from natural causes," Lin suggested.

Glancing sideways at the two women beside her, Libby said, "I don't think so."

Viv was about to ask why it wasn't possible for Maura Wells to have passed away naturally, but Libby held up her hand making a "stop" gesture. "I'm not going to say more. We'll talk later, after you see the body."

Lin's voice sounded wobbly. "Why am I seeing the body?"

"I want you to have a look, see if Maura's spirit is still around. Maybe she can tell you what happened."

"Ghosts don't speak to me," Lin reminded her distant cousin. "They just show up and, well ... try to give me clues about what's bothering them. You can't force them. They do things in their own time and in their own way."

"I know all about it." Libby waved her hand around. "I don't know personally, of course ... I mean I know how the spirits work with you. It can't hurt to have you look around the garden."

"Is the body still in the yard?" Viv asked hoping she would hear an answer in the negative.

"Yes, it is."

Lin and Viv exchanged worried looks as they hurried over the brick sidewalks.

"I can wait until the authorities have removed the body," Lin said.

"It's important for you to be there as soon as possible. It's better not to wait. The spirit may not linger very long."

"We can't just barge in when the police are there," Lin said as they turned onto Gaylord Street.

"Yes, we can," Libby said.

An ambulance and an unmarked police vehicle were parked at the curb of one of the antique houses. Two police cars, one at each end of the street, blocked any other vehicles from entering. Pedestrians were being asked not to walk down the road, but to take an alternate route to their destinations.

The officer at the corner was about to redirect the three women, when he saw Libby. With a nod, the man said, "Ms. Hartnett," and then let them pass.

"Why did he allow us through?" Viv asked with a raised eyebrow.

"I've known Scott since he was a little boy," Libby said.

"But no one is supposed to come down this way," Lin said. "Won't he get into trouble for letting us walk down the road?"

"No," was all Libby said.

When they reached the sidewalk in front of the Colonial home, Lin and Viv could see police photographers taking pictures of the scene and a few other officers moving around the grassy space behind the house looking for any evidence to the contrary that the woman on the bench experienced a natural death.

A sheet covered the dead woman's body.

An older man in a suit noticed them standing beyond the white picket fence that enclosed the front yard and he headed over. He had broad shoulders, white hair, and brown eyes, and moved with an air of authority.

"This is Detective Forrest." Libby made introductions. "He is an old friend of mine." She gestured to her relatives. "This is Carolin Coffin and this is Vivian Coffin. Kin of mine."

The detective shook their hands. "Nice to meet you."

"We'd like to just stand here quietly, if that's okay with you," Libby told the man.

Detective Forrest said, "Stay as long as you need to. I'll ask you to remain outside the fence. Please stay here on the sidewalk." He gave quick nods to Lin and Viv and then he strode away to the rear of the home.

Lin made eye contact with Libby. "He knows you?"

"We've known each other for decades." Libby's eyes scanned the property.

"I mean does he *know* you?" Lin persisted with her question.

"He knows enough." Libby's voice carried a tone

of urgency when she added, "See if you can pick up on anything. See if Maura appears to you."

The three stood without speaking, watching the investigators' process the scene.

With her mind awash in confusion, Lin waited for the chill to envelop her that always accompanied the ghosts. What was the need for her to be at the house? It seemed like this woman had simply passed away. Why was Libby so adamant that Lin try to see Maura's spirit?

Before Lin could clear her mind in order to be open and available to the ghost, other questions popped into her brain. *Why did Maura Wells enter the backyard of this private home and settle down on the garden bench? What was she doing here? Where had she been before going into this garden?*

"Had you been in contact with Ms. Wells?" Lin asked.

Libby looked at her cousin with a disappointed expression. "You don't see anything? You don't see her spirit?"

"Nothing. Can you tell me what you know about the woman?"

Libby let out a sigh. "Anton knew Maura professionally. She was a research historian and worked at a university in Chicago. Maura loved the island and spent many summer weeks here, but she hadn't been back for about five years."

"Why did she stop coming?" Lin asked.

The breeze rustled Libby's silvery bangs. "Responsibilities, commitments. I hadn't talked to Maura for a couple of years. I didn't know her well, we met through Anton. We attended the same charity and fundraising events. We'd talk when we ran into one another."

"How did you know Ms. Wells had died?" Viv asked with a tone of unease. Her arms were wrapped tightly around her body.

"Detective Forrest called me."

"Why?" Lin asked.

"The reason isn't important," Libby said softly.

Lin thought the reason for the detective's call to Libby probably *was* important. "Can you tell us anything else that might be helpful?"

"The only thing that would be helpful is if Maura appeared to you," Libby said. "I'm sorry to have dragged you over here. Thank you for trying, Carolin." The older woman turned and headed away down the sidewalk into town.

"What was this all about?" Viv watched Libby leave. "Does Libby help the police sometimes? What happened to Maura Wells? Why is Libby so interested in the woman's death? She sure didn't tell us much." Viv turned toward her cousin. "Lin?"

Lin had her back to the house where Maura had died and was facing across the street. The air surrounding her was icy cold.

Sebastian Coffin and his wife, Emily, stood shimmering on the opposite sidewalk. They both held Lin's eyes.

Feeling a new sensation of cold at her back, Lin glanced into the yard where the body had been found and had the impression of someone's shadow moving quickly behind the bench Maura had been sitting on. It was gone in a flash. It had to be a ghost, but she knew it wasn't Maura.

Lin's voice was soft when she said to her cousin, "It seems that Libby isn't the only one who is interested in Maura Wells's death."

3

O ne of the innkeepers, Patricia Dellwood, welcomed Libby, island historian and friend, Anton Wilson, and Lin into the nearly two-hundred-year old inn. In the entryway, a beautiful staircase with a finely turned wooden bannister stood to the right. The bed and breakfast had ten guest rooms, some with fireplaces, and two with balconies. Two elegantly-furnished sitting rooms, both with fireplaces, welcomed guests to sit and relax with a glass of wine or sherry.

"I just couldn't believe it when the police told us that one of our guests had passed away," Patricia told them as she led the three visitors to the second floor. "Ms. Wells seemed to be in fine health when I interacted with her."

The innkeeper unlocked one of the doors and opened it. "This was Ms. Wells's room. The police told us they were finished with it so you're free to go in and touch things. I'll be downstairs if you need to ask me anything. Let me know when you're done."

"The woman's belongings have been removed already," Lin said. "What are we looking for?"

"Nothing in particular," Libby said as she moved around the lovely room.

A queen-sized bed was made up with luxurious white linens and a comforter and six fluffy pillows rested against the elegant headboard. A cherrywood desk sat near one wall, two plush chairs were placed by the window, and the bedside table held a small lamp and a vase of fresh flowers.

"It's such a beautiful room," Lin said admiring the furnishings, the artwork, and the small touches that made the space so special.

In his early seventies, Anton, with a thin and wiry build and intelligent eyes that took in every detail, opened the door to the private bath. "Really, Lin, we're not here to write a review of the inn."

"Well, what are we here for? There isn't anything left in here that belonged to Maura Wells. What are we hoping to discover?"

"Just open yourself to what floats on the air, dear." Libby opened and closed the desk drawers.

Lin sat on the edge of the bed and ran her hand over the crisp linens. "It's hard to believe this place used to be a factory."

Anton moved to check the closet. "The old silk factory. Some investors got the idea that the island's climate would be suitable for mulberry bushes to grow here. Mulberry bushes are what the silkworm needs for nourishment. Over four thousand mulberry trees were planted in the Polpis area. Things went well for a time. The business even won a prestigious award at a show in New York City for the quality of their silk fabric."

"So what happened?" Lin asked. "The factory closed after only a few years, didn't it?"

Anton said, "It lasted eight or nine years before the business went under. The mulberry trees failed to thrive. The soil is too sandy here, the climate not ideal."

"How many people worked in the factory?" Lin asked.

"I believe, that initially, twenty women were trained for the work. At its peak, there were as many as fifty women working at the silk production." Anton knelt down and looked under the bed. "It was a very laborious process. There were four spinning machines. They were about twelve feet long, and each one had five hundred bobbins. Each thread had to be wound from the cocoon onto a separate bobbin. The work was complicated."

"What did they make with the silk?"

"Mostly men's clothing items ... silk coats, vests. Things like that," Anton said. "In fact, an ancestor of yours was one of the three incorporators of the silk business."

"Really?" Lin asked. "Who was it?"

"Bradford Coffin," Anton said. "He was a businessman, an investor."

"He must have lost money when the factory went out of business," Lin said.

"It didn't stop him from being successful." Anton pushed himself up from kneeling position.

"Did you find anything under there?"

"Nothing. Not even a speck of dust." Anton walked over to see what Libby was looking at, leaving Lin to her thoughts.

Thinking that the beautiful inn had been once part of a silk factory seemed strange. Women had worked in the building extracting the thread and creating men's fine clothing items with it. The island's economy was faltering back then due to the deteriorating whaling industry and the population of Nantucket had dwindled. Lin thought about the working women of the factory, many whose husbands were probably whalers, out at sea for years at a time.

The temperature around Lin turned cold and she shivered. Some movement at the door caught her eye and she thought she noticed a young woman wearing a long dress hurry past.

Slipping off the bed, Lin walked to the doorway and glanced down the hall. No one was there. No footsteps could be heard.

The room's cool air seemed to get sucked out and away, and the temperature around Lin returned to normal.

"What is it, Carolin?" Libby asked from across the room.

"I thought I saw someone pass by the door." Lin rubbed her hands over her arms to warm them.

"And?" Anton asked.

"Nothing. I was mistaken."

"Too bad," Anton said with a sigh. "I hoped it was Maura. Shall we go then? Unfortunately, visiting Maura's room has proved fruitless."

"Did you think you'd find something here that would explain Ms. Wells's death?" Lin asked as they stepped into the hall and Libby shut the door to the room.

"We hoped we'd find something," Anton told her. "We hoped you might see Maura's ghost."

"She must have crossed over," Lin suggested.

"Perhaps," Libby said.

"Did you know Maura well?" Lin asked Anton.

"Not well. I didn't care for the woman," Anton sniffed. "I don't like to speak ill of the dead, but Maura could be arrogant, dismissive of those whose ideas and research conflicted with her own."

"Then why are you so interested in her death?" Lin asked.

Anton's shoulders fell forward. "There was a note in Maura's hand when she was found. The woman who owns the house and property where Maura was found picked it up and read it. She handed it over to the police."

"What did it say?" Little goosebumps formed over Lin's skin. "Did Maura write the note?"

"It seems she did not," Libby said.

"What was in the note?"

Anton cleared his throat and replied, "It said ... *one down, two to go.*"

Lin's heart began to race. "What does that mean?"

Anton looked over his black eyeglass frames at Lin. "I assume it means two more people will die."

"But," Lin had to swallow hard to remove the tension in her throat. "But, there were no wounds on Maura Wells's body. She wasn't shot or stabbed or strangled. She probably died of natural causes." Lin looked from Anton to Libby. "Didn't she?"

"What about poison?" Anton suggested.

"Poison? You think Ms. Wells was poisoned?" Lin's eyes were wide.

"Keep your voice down," Anton said. "Let's not alarm the guests."

Lin stepped closer to the man. "You think the poison came from this inn?"

"No, we don't," Libby said. "But we do think Maura was poisoned."

"You think she was murdered? You think the note indicates that two more people will be murdered?" Lin felt dizzy and she leaned her back against the wall in the hallway.

"Possibly," Libby gave a quick nod.

"I mentioned earlier that you were descended from one of the owners of the silk factory," Anton said. "There were actually three equal partners who owned the business."

"Yes?" Lin asked. "What about it?"

"On her father's side, Maura was descended from one of the owners," Libby said.

"The note in Maura's hand indicates three deaths will take place," Anton's face was serious.

The meaning finally dawned on Lin and panic raced through her veins. "Three co-owners of the silk factory, so three deaths. Three descendants of the owners will die? Is that what the note might mean? Who was Maura Wells related to?"

"Garrell Williams," Libby said.

"Thomas Samuelson was another founding owner," Anton said.

"And my ancestor, Bradford Coffin, was the third owner." Lin's voice was raspy. "I might be on this person's hit list? And Viv, too?" She looked over to Libby with wide eyes. "Are you related to Bradford Coffin?"

"I am." Libby took in a long breath.

"What is this guy doing?" Lin asked. "Whoever the first relative is he runs into, gets poisoned? Why did he wait for Maura to come back to the island? There must be other people who live here who are related to Garrell Williams. Why was Maura the victim?"

"We don't know," Anton looked down at the floor.

"There are other people who live on-island who are related to Bradford Coffin," Lin spoke barely above a whisper. "How are we going to figure out who's next?"

Libby's face was pale.

"We'll put our heads together," Anton said with forced cheerfulness. "We'll do some research. We'll find the answers we need."

Lin appreciated Anton's optimism, but all she felt was pessimism pulling her down. How would they be able to figure this out? There were too many variables, too many possible victims. "Are the police aware that the note might mean the descendants of the other two silk factory owners could be in danger?"

"They know about our theory," Libby said.

Anton said, "In the meantime, you and Libby and Viv need to be cautious. Don't put a drink down in a bar or a pub or anywhere. Keep your eyes on your food and drinks. Watch out for anyone who might try to tamper with your food or beverages. Stay alert. Don't let your guard down."

Lin gave a slight nod.

"Let's go thank the innkeeper for allowing us access to the room." Libby led the way to the staircase and down to the first floor.

When they reached the bottom of the stairs, Libby and Anton went ahead to find the innkeeper, but Lin stood stock still. Icy air had enveloped her once again.

Turning her head slowly and training her gaze up the stairs to the second floor landing, Lin saw the ghost ... a young woman, in a long, blue dress with a high collar, her golden brown hair brushed up in a bun. The woman's form shimmered as she looked down at Lin and made eye contact with her.

A second later, the ghost began to fade, and she turned abruptly and swished away down the second floor hallway.

Lin knew there was no reason to run up the stairs after her.

The ghost was gone. For now.

4

———

Lin heaved the hydrangea bush into her arms and then placed it gently into the hole her landscaping partner, Leonard Reed, had dug. Once the bush was properly adjusted, the two landscapers filled in soil around the base of the plant.

Nicky snoozed in the grass close to where the work was taking place.

Sitting back on her feet, Lin wiped some sweat from her brow. "And there were three businessmen who started the silk factory and I'm descended from one of them."

While they'd planted the row of ten hydrangeas in their new client's yard, Lin had yammered at Leonard the entire time, telling him about the dead woman on Academy Hill, the inn that used to be a factory, and the ghost she'd seen upstairs at the inn.

"That's quite a story, Coffin," Leonard said as he pulled the hose from the back of the house to water the new bushes. "I heard there was some commotion over on Gaylord Street the other day. Figured the woman had a heart attack or something."

"Maybe she did have a heart attack, but it was probably induced by her being poisoned." Lin rubbed at the soreness in the small of her back. "That's what Libby and Anton think anyway."

"Libby and Anton are usually on the ball about things so I'm inclined to believe their worries are legitimate," Leonard said.

"There was that note in the dead woman's hand, too." Lin gathered up some of the gardening tools. "*One down, two to go.* That's what it said."

"Was the note handwritten or typed?"

Lin looked at the tall, strong, sixty-something-year-old man. "I don't know. I didn't see it. Does it make a difference in some way?"

"Not sure." Leonard shrugged. "So this woman, Maura Wells, was related to one of the owners of the factory and that connection is the reason she was murdered?"

"That's what Libby thinks. I'm not sure I agree."

"The note could back up Libby's thinking," Leonard said. "The words *two to go* mean two more people will die and those victims might be related to the other two factory owners."

Lin nodded. "Am I on the list of possible victims? Is Viv? Or Libby?"

"Or are all three of you on the list and the killer will go after the easiest one to get hold of?"

"Thanks for putting it that way," Lin scowled. "That makes me feel much better."

"You need to think like this nut, whoever it is, so you don't become his victim," Leonard explained. "Another thing to consider is *why*. Why is he killing relatives of the factory owners? What wrong is he avenging? Thinking about motive can help narrow down suspects. If we go by what's written in the note, then only one person related to each man is supposed to die. Those factory owners must be responsible for a wrong committed against the killer's long-ago relative. It's revenge of some sort. An eye for an eye."

Lin frowned. "You know the saying ... an eye for eye makes the whole world blind."

"I don't think the killer cares much about that," Leonard said.

Carrying flowers from the truck to the gardens

behind the house, the landscapers got to work putting the blooms in place. Nicky followed them and found a comfortable spot in the shade where he could supervise the job.

"You need to think about your safety, Coffin."

"Oh, I am," Lin said kneeling next to the garden plot. "Sometimes, it's all I think about. It's a terrible thought to feel like someone is out there watching me."

"Did anyone who worked at the factory die in an accident?" Leonard asked.

"I don't know. I haven't looked into it yet. Anton is researching trying to find some link. Viv and I are meeting with him this evening."

"Maybe those factory owners did something to hurt someone financially," Leonard speculated.

"That's a good idea." Lin used a trowel to dig some holes for the flowers. "Maybe someone was ruined financially by the three factory owners. Maybe the thing being avenged doesn't even have anything to do with the silk factory itself. Maybe it's the three men who formed the business. They must have invested in other things together besides the factory."

"The place went out of business in less than ten years," Leonard thought aloud. "There could have been someone who lost money due to the factory's closing and the relative blames the factory owners for ruining that person's life."

"That's reason to kill? After so many years?" Lin asked. "It was almost two hundred years ago."

"Stranger things have happened." Leonard tugged some flowers from their containers. "Especially on this island."

"Maybe the police will sort it all out." Lin moved further down the garden bed.

"What about the ghost you saw in the inn?" Leonard asked. "You think she's from the mid 1800s?"

"I get that impression. The way she wears her hair, the clothes she has on. Maybe she worked in the factory?" Lin guessed.

"Why is the ghost appearing to you?"

"To warn me of danger?" Lin offered. "I also saw Sebastian and Emily standing outside the inn on the sidewalk."

Leonard lifted his head and turned to his partner with an expression of worry. "Both of them?"

"Yes."

"Huh." Leonard stared at the flowers, thinking. "Well."

"Well, what?" Lin looked up from her planting. "Do you have an idea?"

"Not an idea, really. I was just wondering ... if Marguerite knows what's going on."

Leonard's wife, Marguerite, died a number of years ago and she had not yet crossed over. Her spirit remained in the house she'd shared with Leonard, and although he was able to see her, his wife's ghost never uttered a word to him.

"You think she knows what's going on with other spirits?" Lin asked with excitement in her voice. "Can you ask her?"

"I will ask her." Leonard gave a nod. "Can't promise anything."

"I know, but it's worth a shot."

Leonard gently tamped some soil around the flowers he'd just planted. "So the questions are ... what's the killer's motivation? Why is he killing now? Who is the ghost-woman at the inn? What is she trying to tell you?"

"You forgot one other question," Lin said. "Who's next?"

Leonard did not want to give that question any thought. "What do you know about the dead woman ... Maura Wells?"

"Not a whole lot. She was a professor of history,

a researcher at a university in the Chicago area. Anton didn't like her much. He said she was arrogant."

"The pot calling the kettle black?" Leonard's lips turned up into a smile thinking that many people might say the same thing about Anton. "Was Ms. Wells on-island to do some research?"

Lin sat back on the grass and Nicky crawled over so she could scratch his ears. "I wonder. If she *was* here researching, did that set things in motion? Did her research stir up something that should have been left alone?"

"Anton should look into that," Leonard suggested. He pulled two bottles of water from the cooler and handed one of them to Lin. Before sipping from his bottle, he took out the doggie bowl from the cooler and filled it for the dog. "What thing could Maura Wells have come across that instigated someone to commit murder? How long had she been here?"

"I think Libby told me Ms. Wells had been here for only a week."

"Do you know how long she planned to stay?"

"A month."

"Someone moved fast," Leonard noted. "Someone found out pretty quick that Ms. Wells was here. Was she going to stay for a month at the inn? That would have been expensive."

"Libby said Ms. Wells was moving in a couple of days to a house she'd rented for three weeks."

Leonard took an apple from the cooler. "Why don't you stay with Viv for a while."

Nicky had rolled onto his back so his owner could rub his tummy. "You're scaring me," Lin said to her partner.

"You need to be careful, Coffin. I've got extra bedrooms. If you and Viv want to come to my place for a while, you're welcome to stay. That little, brown hound of yours can come, too."

Nicky jumped up, hurried over to the man, licked his face, then plopped down in his lap.

Leonard wiped at his cheek to remove the dog kiss. "Maybe I better rethink the dog's invitation."

"What about Queenie? Are you fine with a cat in your house?"

"The more, the merrier." Leonard bit into the apple. "As long as none of you mind a ghost in the house."

"Marguerite wouldn't mind?" Lin asked.

"Nah. She likes you. She thinks your friendship has been good for me." Leonard patted Nicky's head. "Of course, I always tell her she's wrong about that."

"I'll talk to Viv about it. Maybe we can take turns staying at each other's house, then we wouldn't have to barge in on you."

"Suit yourselves. The door is always open." Leonard narrowed his eyes. "You put me on speed dial, Coffin. Anything worries you, you call me right away."

"You think this is a big deal, don't you?" Lin sighed. "I've been trying to downplay it, but I've woken up the past two nights in a cold sweat."

Leonard tried to calm Lin's fears. "Listen, there are lots of descendants of the Coffins on this island. The odds are that this killer doesn't even know you exist."

Lin cocked her head to one side. "You and I run a well-known Nantucket landscaping business. Most people here know who we are." When her phone buzzed, Lin pulled it out of her back pocket. "It's a text from Anton."

She turned the phone so Leonard could read the message.

Where are you? I have some news. I need to see you. Now.

5

L in was waiting at the front of their client's house when Anton pulled to the curb in his small, light blue car. Leonard had taken the truck and gone on to the next client's place.

"I'll take the dog with me," Leonard had said. "Have Anton drop you off when he's finished talking to you."

Anton waved Lin around to the passenger seat.

"Where are we going?" Lin she shut the door and buckled her seat belt. "I thought you only wanted to talk to me."

"Another person has been attacked." Anton hit the gas.

Lin nearly choked.

"A man," Anton said. "Poisoned. He was out for lunch with two of his friends. When they were at the bar, he keeled over, unconscious. He is at the hospital."

"He lived?" Lin asked hopefully.

"He was alive when Libby contacted me. The man is in serious condition."

Lin had to hold onto the grab bar on the door when Anton took the turn going too fast. "Who is he? He's related to this case?"

"His name is Warren Topper. He and his wife have a house here. They use it in the summer, the rest of the year they live in New York."

"Is he related to one of the men who owned the silk factory?"

"We are assuming so, but we don't know for sure. Libby is at the hospital right now. The police have cleared her to speak with Mrs. Topper."

"The police know that Libby has some ... powers?"

"Detective Forrest knows. He keeps it to himself. The rest of law enforcement knows nothing. Forrest and Libby were both born on-island and have lived here their whole lives. The man has had some inter-actions with ghosts. He knew Lilianna as well."

A life-long resident of Nantucket, Lilianna had passed away not long ago. The woman was in her nineties ... at least. Lilianna had powers and was able to see ghosts. She'd helped Detective Forrest with cases from time to time.

"Does he know about me?" Lin asked in a soft voice. She didn't like the idea that someone outside of her circle of family and friends knew about her skill.

"Don't worry. Libby wouldn't say anything to Forrest about you. If you're seen with Libby, however, he probably suspects that you work with her. You don't need to be concerned about Detective Forrest, Carolin. He only asks what needs to be asked. He doesn't pry. He is a private man who allows others their privacy."

"Okay." Lin saw the hospital up ahead and braced herself for Anton's wild turn into the driveway. She gave Anton a look out of the corner of her eye. "I should have had Leonard drive me over here. I wouldn't have been afraid for my life if he was doing the driving."

"Very funny," Anton muttered as he pulled the vehicle into a parking spot. "You have arrived in one piece."

When they entered the hospital, Libby was in the waiting room. She stood up when she saw them and herded them outside to sit on a bench that had been placed under a shade tree. "Better out here where I can speak freely."

"How is Mr. Topper?" Lin asked.

Libby said, "Still unconscious. He was at the new restaurant down by the docks with two friends. He's been checked for heart attack and stroke and both are negative. The police suspect poisoning. They're waiting for confirmation from the lab."

"Were you able to speak with Topper's wife?" Lin asked.

"Briefly," Libby said. "The men Topper was with are good friends of the couple. They've known each other for years. I doubt they had anything to do with the poisoning."

"Where was Mr. Topper before he met his friends at the restaurant?"

"He was at home. Mrs. Topper is unsure if he made any stops before heading to lunch."

"Was there a note?" Lin's stomach clenched.

"No note this time." Libby shook her head.

"Do you know yet if Mr. Topper was related to any of the silk factory owners?"

"Anton is going to look into that. When I asked

the wife that question, she looked at me like I was crazy. I didn't bother explaining Maura's death to the woman. She is understandably distraught. The police can handle telling her the details of Maura Wells's murder."

"What about Maura?" Lin asked. "Was poison found in her system?"

Libby said, "The medical examiner's results were consistent with poisoning. It was a fairly fast-acting toxin that would result in death in thirty to forty-five minutes after ingesting it."

"Where was Maura before she ended up dead in the garden of a private home?" Lin questioned.

"That has not yet been determined," Libby said.

After leaving the hospital, Anton drove Lin to her cottage and Viv met them there. When Leonard arrived to drop off the dog before heading home, Lin gave him an update on what had happened. Viv was brought up to speed about the latest victim and that poison had been used to kill Maura Wells.

A look of horror washed over Viv's face as her hand flew to her throat. "It really *was* poison that killed Ms. Wells."

"After ingestion, this particular poison would have been effective within about thirty minutes," Anton informed Viv.

"Someone at the inn could have poisoned Maura," Lin speculated. "She may have had something to drink, then went out for a walk, became ill, spotted the bench, becoming disoriented, and headed into the garden to sit down."

"We need to find out where she was before becoming ill," Viv said. "How long was Mr. Topper at the restaurant before he passed out?"

Lin looked at Anton for the answer.

"I believe the man met his friends, the three of them went to the bar and ordered drinks," Anton said. "The men chatted and enjoyed the beverages for about fifteen minutes before Topper began to show some signs of distress."

"Someone at the bar could have slipped the poison into Topper's drink," Viv suggested.

"That's true," Lin said. "But Topper might have ingested the poison prior to his arrival at the restaurant. The dosage wasn't enough to kill him so maybe it didn't act as fast as it would have if he'd had a higher dosage."

"That is a complication," Anton told them. "Topper may have had something to drink before arriving at the restaurant ... and that drink may have contained the poison. It may not have been the drink he ordered at the bar that poisoned him."

"Can't tests be run on the glass Topper was using to see if traces of poison are in it?" Lin asked.

"I've heard the glass can't be found." Anton sighed. "It broke when Topper collapsed and during clean-up, it went into the trash. The trash has been combed through and the glass was not found."

Viv rolled her eyes. "Nothing can be easy, can it?"

Lin prepared tomato soup, grilled cheese sandwiches, and salad for dinner and when the meal was finished, the three amateur sleuths gathered around Anton's laptop on the kitchen table to do some research.

Anton tapped away at the keyboard. "I'm in a database of family histories and ancestral lines. If Warren Topper has been added previously to the data, then his lineage will come up. Otherwise, it will take some work to find out if the man is related to Thomas Samuelson, the third factory owner, or perhaps, to Bradford Coffin. It took me a good amount of time to confirm that Maura Wells was a descendent of Garrell Williams."

"Is there any information about something bad happening long ago in the factory?" Viv asked. "An accident? A death?"

"Not that I've found yet." Anton adjusted his glasses to better see the laptop screen.

Viv sat up and turned to her cousin. "Do you still have those old newspapers Leonard gave you a while back?"

Lin's eyes went wide. "Yes. I put the box away in the guest bedroom. I'll get them." In a few minutes, the young woman had returned to the kitchen carrying a huge box filled with old newspapers and books of collected newspaper editions. "We can look at the old newspaper articles from the mid-1800s. Maybe there will be a story reporting trouble at the factory."

The cousins separated the articles and books according to date and split between them the stories from the time period they were interested in.

Settling in for a couple of hours of searching, Lin said, "At least when Mr. Topper is feeling better, he can tell us where he was before going to the restaurant to meet his friends. He can tell us who he interacted with and if he had something to drink before arriving at the bar."

"That will be a huge help," Viv nodded as she turned a page of one of the books.

"The man may not recall the details of his day leading up to his collapse," Anton said without looking up. "Topper may not be the person he was prior to the poisoning."

"How do you mean?" Viv asked.

"Poisoning can cause brain damage. Topper could emerge from his coma-like state with some issues ... memory problems, trouble comprehending and producing language, motor issues, difficulties with cognition, mood problems."

"Really? Gosh." Viv stared across the room at nothing. "I thought he'd wake up and everything would be fine."

"We'll have to wait and see," Anton said. "Time will tell."

"Here's an article about the building of the factory," Lin said. "The founders of the silk company were in such a rush to complete the structure, that during construction, they supported the building with barrels because the ground was frozen. The real foundation didn't go in until after the ground thawed in the spring."

"Why were they in such a rush?" Viv asked.

"Probably because they wanted to start making money," Lin told her. *Money.* Was money the reason for Maura Wells's death and the attack on Mr. Topper?

Anton's phone vibrated and he picked it up to read the message. Viv and Lin heard him let out a long sigh before he raised his head and made eye contact with the cousins.

"Mr. Topper has passed away."

Lin's heart skipped a beat.

Two down, one to go.

6

It was a warm, sunny, late afternoon when Lin and Jeff rode their bikes for six miles on the paved bicycle path to the town of Madaket at the western end of the island. Passing green fields, wooded parcels of land, and the occasional house, they stopped at the town's restaurant to pick up some sandwiches to eat on the beach.

Parking and locking their bikes, the young couple carried their backpacks and dinner down to the white sand beach with the blue ocean stretching out before them under the perfect sky. Some gulls cawed as they sailed overhead and the cresting waves shot white bubbles and foam into the air as they broke against the sand.

"Look at the water," Lin said with a smile as she

pulled a small blanket from her backpack and spread it over the sand. "Let's jump in before we eat."

The surf at Madaket could be strong and swift and swimmers had to take care not to be caught in fast-moving current.

After removing two towels from his pack, Jeff pulled off his t-shirt and tossed it on the blanket. "Let's ride some waves, but let's not go out too far. We don't want to get caught in an undercurrent and have a hard time swimming back to shore."

Lin and Jeff dashed into the waves laughing and jumping and spent the next twenty minutes body surfing in the ocean until Jeff announced he was hungry. Returning to the blanket, they toweled off, sat down, and dug into the sandwiches they'd purchased before arriving at the beach.

"That was great. The waves were terrific and the water was warm," Lin said, biting into her sandwich.

"And this meatball and sausage sandwich is delicious." Jeff licked his lower lip to remove a bit of sauce.

"Look at the sky," Lin said.

The sun was low in the sky painting the blue background with pinks, violets, and splashes of red. Madaket was known for gorgeous sunsets as the big yellow-orange ball of fire made its dramatic evening plunge into the sea.

Jeff put his arm around Lin's shoulders and drew her close. "Perfect."

When they finished their dinner, the two decided to take a walk along the beach, and as they strolled, Lin brought Jeff up-to-date on the latest case.

"It's terrible," Jeff said. "I'm very sorry Mr. Topper passed away. And without regaining consciousness. Too bad he wasn't able to give an account of where he'd been just prior to arriving at the bar."

"The whole thing is shocking," Lin agreed. "It would have been a big help to hear if he'd had something to eat or drink before meeting with his friends. We might have been able to determine if the poison was ingested while Mr. Topper drank at the bar or maybe, before he arrived."

"His wife might be able to help with that information," Jeff said.

"Libby has arranged for Viv and I to speak with Mrs. Topper tomorrow. I'm surprised the woman agreed, but she must want to do what she can to help find her husband's killer."

"Has Anton figured out if Topper is related to any of the silk factory owners?" Jeff asked.

Lin shook her head. "Not yet. There's a good amount of information to wade through."

"Why do Libby and Anton think these deaths are related to the silk factory?" Jeff reached down for a small stone and skipped it far out into the ocean.

Lin explained, "Libby doesn't say much about that, but Anton let it slip that Maura Wells was working on a book about the island's economy back in the day. I guess they both think that Maura's digging into the past may have triggered someone to take revenge for something. And the note that was found in Maura's hand insinuated that there would be three murders in total. There were three owners of the factory so it seemed plausible that the people being killed might have ties to those factory owners. It's still just a theory."

"Maybe the murders have nothing to do with the men who owned the factory," Jeff offered.

"I've been wondering that myself." Lin picked up a cream-colored shell and, for a moment, held it up to admire the light shimmering against it. "But at least, attempting to tie the victims to the owners is a place to start."

"Did something bad happen in the factory?" Jeff asked. "Have you found anything to suggest a death or an accident took place in the building?"

"Not yet." Lin squeezed her boyfriend's hand. "We don't have much to go on, do we?"

"Give it time," Jeff said encouragingly. "Tell me about the ghost you saw at the inn."

"It was a brief appearance," Lin said. "The ghost was a woman, in her mid-twenties maybe, wearing a long dress with a high collar. Her hair was in a bun. I saw her rush by the guest room where Maura Wells had been staying and I saw her at the top of the stairs when we were leaving the inn."

"Did she seem like she wanted to communicate with you?"

"She held my eyes for a long time. Her face was serious. I can't say what emotions she might have been feeling, but her gaze was intense. She wants me to know something, but what it is, I can't say."

Jeff smiled. "You'll figure it out."

Lin and Jeff rode the bikes back to town, took showers and changed at Lin's house, played with Nicky for a while, and then walked into the historic district to stroll past the shops and have a drink at the outside bar down by the docks.

Walking along the brick sidewalks under the streetlamps, they stopped at a few store windows to look in at the wares, sat on a bench for a while to listen to a violinist playing songs on a corner, strolled past a long line of people waiting to get ice cream at a popular shop, and then continued along Broad Street to take a right on Easy Street.

Passing a small antiques store, Jeff tugged on Lin's arm. "Let's have a look. I'd like a painting of a ship or a seascape for my living room. A friend of mine told me the prices are decent here."

Lin had never been inside the old shop. The display tables and walls held all sorts of beautiful objects ... ship's wheels, sailors' valentines, paintings, clocks, barometers, old books, photographs, dishes and teacups, jewelry, tide clocks, lightship baskets, desks, tables, and hutches.

"How have I not visited this place before?" Lin asked as they moved slowly around admiring the things. "I'll have to bring Viv here."

Lin and Jeff stopped to look at two nautical paintings hanging on one wall.

"I think I like this one." Jeff pointed at a painting of a storm at sea.

"I don't know," Lin said. "It's beautiful, but it scares me. The ship looks like it's going to sink."

Jeff chuckled. "How about the other one then? I don't want you to be uncomfortable every time you're in my living room."

Lin said with a smile, "Get the one you like best. I'll get used to it."

While Jeff stared at the paintings trying to make a decision, Lin wandered around the store and discovered a small bookcase filled with volumes on island history. Taking out one of the books, she turned the pages and became engrossed in the tales of old Nantucket.

Turning the next page, she saw several old photographs of the town, the docks, and houses from different parts of the island ... from magnificent captains' homes to small, tidy cottages. Some of the pictures were from the mid to late 1800s showing townspeople and sailors and shopkeepers.

"Lin, I think I'm going to get this one," Jeff called to her.

Heading back to where Jeff stood, Lin asked him which one he'd chosen.

"This one of the sailing ship. The sea is calm and the sky is blue. It's calming, not frightening," he kidded his girlfriend.

"Good choice."

"I'm going to have them hold it for me until tomorrow so I don't have to carry it around town."

When Jeff went to get the salesclerk, Lin meandered around the store and ended up back near the bookshelf. One of the pages of the book she'd left out on the table was fluttering slightly from the breeze of the overhead ceiling fan and Lin walked over to return it to the shelf.

The photographs on the page caught her attention and she leaned forward to get a better look. One was of an inn, another of a ship sailing past Brant Point. Moving her eyes over the page, Lin noticed a photograph of the old hat factory.

Turning the page, she saw a building with a group of about twenty-five women standing in front of it. All of the women wore long dresses and had their hair pinned back or held up in buns. Their facial expressions were serious.

"Are you ready to go?" Jeff came up behind Lin and she almost jumped when he placed his hand on her back.

"Look at these old photographs," she said to Jeff. "Some of them are from the 1840s."

Jeff looked down at the open book and pointed. "This is Main Street. It really hasn't changed much at all."

The little hairs on Lin's arms stood up and a shiver of cold air washed over her. Slowly lifting her head, she turned slightly to look around the shop expecting to see a spirit. The sensation of chill disappeared and she thought maybe the ceiling fans had made her feel cool.

Just as she was about to close the book, Lin's eyes fell onto a photo of a group of women standing in front of a building.

She snatched up the book from the table and stared at the picture.

"Jeff." Lin whispered.

"What is it?" He glanced over her shoulder.

"This woman. This one." Lin gently touched the page of the book with a shaking finger. "Right here." With her heart pounding, she said softly, "This is my ghost."

7

―――――

Lin brought along the old book she'd purchased in the antique store so that Viv could see the picture of the group of women workers standing in front of the silk factory.

"That's her, on the right, next to the tall woman." Lin removed one hand from the steering wheel and gestured.

Viv held the book in her lap and stared at the woman in the black and white photo. "I'd say she's in her mid-twenties. Her hair is light. She looks intelligent. I can't tell if she's wearing a wedding ring or not."

"No one's name is listed. It only says, employees of the Island Silk Factory."

"You're sure it's her?" Viv still scrutinized the picture.

Lin turned the truck onto upper Main Street and passed large houses set back from the street. "Absolutely. No doubt in my mind. It says the photo was taken in 1842."

"The ghost has only appeared to you once." Viv looked out through the windshield. "You need to see more of her to get a sense of what she wants from you."

"Maybe she doesn't want anything from me."

Viv gave her cousin a look of skepticism. "Wishful thinking." Watching the trees and brush and homes as they passed, she added, "Why won't the ghost-woman show up wherever you are? Is she shy?"

"Maybe she doesn't want to leave the inn," Lin offered.

"Why wouldn't she?" Viv questioned.

"She might feel safe there."

"In the place she used to work?" Viv squinted in question. "Isn't that odd? To want to remain in the place where you used to work?"

"For whatever reason, this woman stays in the inn and doesn't cross over," Lin said and then frowned. "I'd like to see her again. I get the feeling that seeing her would help with these poisoning cases."

"Well," Viv said, her eyes bright with an idea. "How about we stay at the inn overnight? You've already visited the room where Maura Wells stayed. I don't think the innkeeper would want you hanging around there without reason. We don't have any business in the place, at least not business we can discuss with the inn's owner. We can't say, *Oh, hi. We want to sit in the living room so we can interact with the ghost who stays here.*" Viv shook her head. "But if we booked a room for one night, it would give you the access you need without having to provide an explanation for wanting to be there."

"It's a great idea. Let's do that. I hope they have a vacancy available soon." Lin turned into a long driveway and pulled to a stop next to the huge home's three-car garage.

"I'm not looking forward to this." Viv appeared to sink into the passenger seat.

"It's never easy talking with someone who recently lost a loved one. Come on, let's get it done." Lin opened the door and slipped out of her truck onto the crushed, white shell driveway.

The house, newly-shingled, was enormous with a wide covered porch running along the front. A long bed of flowering hydrangeas had been planted next to the home. With her tail thumping against the porch floor, a big black Labrador slowly pushed herself up from its nap and walked down the few steps to greet them.

The front door opened and Mrs. Topper emerged. "The dog's name is Rolly. She's as friendly as can be. I'm watching her today for my friend. Would you like me to call her away from you?" The woman was slim, average height, in her mid-fifties, with her blond hair cut into a chin-length bob.

"Oh, no. We both like dogs," Lin informed Mrs. Topper as she patted the head and neck of the Lab.

"I'm Maggie Willard Topper." She shook hands with the cousins and they introduced themselves and offered condolences before heading into the elegant, but comfortably furnished living room. Three light blue sofas had been grouped in front of a fireplace with views to the outside through nearly floor-to-ceiling windows on two sides of the room.

Lin thanked the woman for seeing them. "I know the police must have asked you many of the same questions we'll bring up, but I hope you can bear with us."

Maggie Topper nodded, her lips tight and her face serious.

"Do you know if your husband stopped off somewhere between the time he left the house and when he met his friends at the restaurant's bar?" Lin asked.

"I don't know if he stopped anywhere else or not." Maggie touched her hair and pushed it away from her face. "He always took the car to the lot on Washington Street and parked, then he'd walk around town from there. I assume he did the same thing as he always did, since the police located his car in the lot."

"Was the condition of the car the same as when Mr. Topper left the house?" Viv asked.

Maggie sat up straighter. "Yes. At least, I didn't notice anything out of the ordinary. Why would you ask about the car?"

"We wondered if someone might have approached Mr. Topper in the lot," Lin said. "We were interested to know if they'd been anything to indicate that your husband might have tussled with someone."

"I don't think so." Maggie held her hands tightly together in her lap.

"When Mr. Topper went into town, did he have a routine of any kind?" Viv asked. "Did he frequent the same stores and establishments? Did he have a friend he might have stopped in to say hello to?"

"Warren was meeting his two friends at the restaurant," Maggie said. "I doubt he would have stopped anywhere else. He must have parked in the public lot and strolled to the restaurant."

"There was no one in town he might have popped in to say hello to?" Lin asked.

"I can't think of anyone." Maggie's bottom lip twitched slightly. "We have an accountant and a lawyer in town who we use from time to time, but Warren had no reason to call on them."

"How did your husband seem recently?" Lin questioned. "Did he seem out of sorts? Sad, depressed? Was he worried about anything?"

Maggie shook her head. "He was himself. He never gave any hint that something might be wrong." The woman blinked back tears. "Who would kill Warren? Poison him? It's like something out of a terrible, old movie."

Lin murmured something understanding and kind ... feeling inadequate, as usual, in her ability to offer some comforting words.

Viv asked, "Your husband was in good health?"

"He was. He'd recently had his annual physical and he passed with flying colors."

"He was a banker?" Viv questioned.

Maggie nodded. "An investment banker and financial advisor."

"He was still working?"

"Yes, I didn't see Warren retiring any time soon. He enjoyed his work. The past few summers, he took time from the office and worked from his den here in the house. When he needed to go in, he flew from the airport to New York and returned the same way."

"How long have you been coming to the island?" Lin asked.

"Oh, gosh, forever. This house has been in the family for almost two hundred years."

"Did your husband have connections to Nantucket?"

"No, we came here together for the first time when we started dating. He loved the island."

"Did Mr. Topper have any relatives who were from the island? An ancestor, perhaps?" Viv asked.

"An ancestor? From Nantucket?" Maggie seemed surprised by the question. "No. Warren's family was from the mainland."

"Did the police ask you this same question?" Lin asked.

"No, they didn't. Why would that be important?"

"Just wondering about connections, that's all."

"Is the name Thomas Samuelson familiar to you?" Viv asked. "Did Mr. Topper ever mention someone of that name being a relative? As a great-great-grandfather, perhaps?"

"I don't believe so. I never heard the name."

"What about Bradford Coffin or Garrell Williams? Do those names sound familiar at all?" Lin questioned.

"Coffin? Your last names are Coffin. I know that people with that surname were some of the first families to come to the island, but in relation to Warren or me? Not at all," Maggie said. "What was the other name?"

Lin repeated it for the woman.

"Garrell? No, I've never heard that name before."

"Did your husband know a woman named Maura Wells?"

Maggie's eyes flashed. "That was the name of the woman who was poisoned a few days ago. Warren didn't know her. When we heard about Ms. Wells being poisoned, we discussed what reason someone could have to kill the poor woman. If Warren knew her, he would have said so."

"Do you have any idea why someone would want to hurt Warren?" Lin asked. "Any business problems? Any issues or arguments with someone?"

Maggie shook her head and batted at her eyes. "He never said any such thing. Everything was the way it always was."

"Was there any place in town that Mr. Topper liked to go? A particular store? A café?"

Maggie was about to shake her head, but then said, "Warren liked to stop at that bookstore on Main Street, *Viv's Victus*. He liked their coffee. He liked browsing the shelves for something to read."

Lin's and Viv's jaws almost dropped.

"Wait," Maggie said eyeing Viv, recognition registering on her face. "Aren't you the owner of that bookstore?"

Viv cleared her throat. "I am. Your husband liked to drop in?"

"He did. Whenever he went into town, he often stopped in."

"Did Mr. Topper go into town a little early that day?" Lin asked. "Would he have had time to visit the bookstore before meeting his friends?"

"I wasn't here when he left the house," Maggie told them. "I was at a friend's house in Cisco. I'm not sure if Warren left early for town or not."

After a few more questions, Lin and Viv thanked the woman for her time and left the house. Walking to Lin's truck, Viv said, "Warren Topper did not get poisoned in my store."

"Let's hope not anyway," Lin said.

Viv glared at her cousin. "It would be impossible. It's me, Mallory, and three others who would have made Topper's drink. Those employees have worked with me for a long time. None of them would have any reason to poison that man. Anyway, why would Topper stop in for a drink when he was headed to a bar a few blocks away to meet his friends?"

"You're right. That really doesn't sound plausible," Lin asked. "You don't recall ever seeing Topper in the bookstore?"

"Not from a grainy photo that was on the news. I'll look at some of the photos again. If he was a regular, I'd most likely remember him." Viv yanked the passenger side door open using too much effort. "And it doesn't sound like Topper is descended from anyone who lived on Nantucket. At least not any of the silk factory owners."

Lin said, "We'll see if Anton finds a link that Mr. Topper didn't know about. If he doesn't find anything, then that shoots down Libby's and Anton's theory that the killer is exacting revenge for something the three owners did so long ago."

"If that turns out to be the case," Viv asked. "Where do we go from here?"

Lin was quiet as she turned on the truck's engine and steered it down the driveway. "To stay overnight at the Seaborne Inn."

8

L in and Viv were shown to a room with two twin beds and a private bath on the second floor of the inn. The beds were covered with luxurious linens, plenty of fluffy pillows, and comforters as soft as clouds.

Patricia, the innkeeper said, "Remember there is wine and sherry in the living room along with some hors d'oeuvres and cake at 5pm. The breakfast tomorrow morning is from 7am to 10am and is served in the dining room. You're welcome to take your breakfasts to your room or to the sitting rooms or out to the gardens. Let me know if I can be of any help."

When the woman left, Viv plopped down onto her bed on her back and closed her eyes. "This bed is so comfortable. No wonder the ghost-woman never leaves this building."

Smiling at Viv, Lin sat on her bed and ran her hand over the comforter. "When I was here the other day, I couldn't believe how soft the comforter was."

Viv opened one eye. "Soft as silk? As in a silk factory?"

"Very funny," Lin deadpanned.

"It's hard to believe this beautiful, relaxing place was once a factory where people worked all day." Viv pushed herself up. "I had a good idea to come stay here for the night, didn't I? It's a little after 5pm. Let's go downstairs and enjoy a glass of wine. Maybe your ghost will join us."

Five guests holding wine glasses stood around chatting with the two innkeepers, Patricia and Milton Dellwood. In her sixties with short blond hair and bright blue eyes, Patricia smiled at Lin and Viv, poured them glasses of cabernet, pointed out the afternoon hors d'oeuvres, and introduced them to the other guests. "Lin is a landscaper here on the island and Viv owns the bookstore on Main Street. They're cousins."

An older man with a full white mustache raised an eyebrow. "If you live on-island, why stay here at the inn?"

"Once in a while, a person needs to de-stress," Viv smiled sweetly. "We run businesses here so it isn't easy to get away. Now and then my cousin and I enjoy a night away from our usual routines and the lovely inns on-island offer a beautiful and relaxing change of pace."

"That makes a lot of sense." An older woman came up beside the man who asked the question. "A night away, a mini getaway, but without all the fuss and bother of traveling. What a smart thing to do. And in such wonderful surroundings. You must return to your responsibilities feeling quite refreshed."

While the older couple questioned Viv about her bookshop, Patricia asked Lin, "Is everything fine with your room?"

"Yes, it's great, thank you."

"I was surprised to see you again. When you were here last, did visiting Maura Wells's room prove helpful?"

"Unfortunately, not," Lin said. "We didn't find anything that could help the investigation."

"Too bad." Patricia topped off her glass of merlot. "I hope the police can solve the case quickly."

Lin wanted to move the conversation to something other than Maura Wells's murder so she asked, "How long have you owned the inn?"

"Oh, gosh," Patricia said. "Nearly twenty-five years. Time really does fly. We married young and had our two kids right away. Once they went off to college, we decided to move here, buy the inn, and become innkeepers."

"Were you innkeepers before moving here?" Lin asked.

"Oh, no." Patricia chuckled. "Milton was a partner in a law firm and I was a financial analyst. When we got here, we didn't know what we were doing. We had to learn pretty darned fast."

"The house is beautiful," Lin told her.

"You know its history?" Patricia asked.

"A little. The building was once a silk factory?"

"That's right. When the factory went out of business, the building was eventually divided into two residences. For a while, this side was a boarding house, then it was turned into an inn. The other side of the building has been a residential home for over a hundred and fifty years." Patricia picked up a small mushroom turnover. "Have you met our resident ghost yet?"

Lin almost paled. "What?"

The older woman who was talking with Viv

heard Patricia's comment and looked over. "Patricia has been claiming a ghost lives here for years. I've never once seen her. I think Pat invented the whole thing to make the inn seem like an intriguing place. It isn't necessary to make up a story. Some people wouldn't want to stay here if they thought a ghost lived here. The inn is fabulous as it is. It doesn't need a crazy story about a ghost." She turned back to listen to what her husband and Viv were discussing.

"She's wrong," Patricia whispered. "There *is* a ghost." When she saw the look on Lin's face, she quickly asked, "Does that bother you?"

"What? No. No, it doesn't. It just surprised me." Lin took a long swallow of her wine.

"Oh, don't worry. The ghost is quiet, not scary or anything like that."

"You've seen this ghost?" Lin asked.

"I sure have. My husband has, too. It's a woman. I believe she's from the time the factory was in operation."

"Why do you think that?" Lin's heart raced. She wanted to know if Patricia could see the same ghost she saw.

"Just a feeling I have."

"What does she look like?" Lin asked.

"She wears a long dress with a high collar and

her hair is up in a bun. I never really have gotten a good look at her face. She zips by so fast."

"Is she solid?" Lin questioned.

Viv heard a few pieces of Lin's and Patricia's conversation and glanced over at her cousin with a raised eyebrow.

Lin shrugged.

"Solid?" Patricia asked and gave it some thought. "No, she isn't solid like we are. I'm not sure how to describe her. It's like a wisp of smoke when she moves past. I get a sense of her, but I can't make out her features."

"When do you see her? Every day? At regular times?"

"Not every day." Patricia shook her head. "Once every couple of months or so."

"Is there anything going on at the time that makes her appear?"

"I never thought about that." Patricia tapped her index finger against her chin.

"Do you experience any sensations when she shows up?" Lin asked.

"Like what? Noises? A cold breeze?" Patricia let out a chuckle. "I think that stuff about cold air when a ghost shows up is foolishness, but maybe I hear a soft rustling just before she zooms by."

Lin could definitely refute what the woman was saying about cold air arriving before a ghost appears, but she decided she wouldn't mention anything about it. "A rustling?" she asked.

"Like fabric swishing," Patricia said. "I was interviewed once about it for a book a woman was doing about ghosts and spirits of Nantucket. There are supposed to be a lot of haunted places on the island. Some ghosts are mean or frightening. Thankfully, our ghost is calm and gentle. I couldn't stay in a house that had a nasty spirit."

A few more guests came down the stairs and entered the living room. Before Patricia moved away to the buffet table to pour drinks for the newcomers, Lin asked, "Do you know her name?"

Patricia looked confused at first, but then her expression cleared. "The ghost-woman? No, I don't."

"Do you get any feelings about her? Why she stays here?" Lin asked.

"No. I wondered about that. Why doesn't she move on? It seems kind of sad." The innkeeper went to help the new guests with drinks.

Viv sidled up next to her cousin and used a soft voice when she asked, "Was she talking to you about ghosts?"

"Just one ghost. The one that lives in this building." Lin kept her voice quiet as she relayed what Patricia had told her.

"Is it the same one you saw?" Viv looked nervously over her shoulders. "Maybe it wasn't such a great idea to stay overnight here."

"It sounds like the same ghost." Suddenly, the air around Lin became icy cold and she glanced around trying to locate the source.

The ghost-woman appeared across the room, standing very still next to the baby grand piano and making eye contact with Lin. A beautiful diamond-cut silver necklace graced the ghost's neck and she wore a long, light blue dress. Her form was translucent and her atoms sparkled and shimmered to emit a gentle glow.

Lin ran her hand over her arms to banish the goosebumps and then moved her eyes to Patricia to see if the woman noticed that someone unexpected was in the room with them. Patricia poured wine and chatted with the guests unaware of the shimmering spirit.

Lin looked back to the ghost. A painful sadness came off of the spirit and the feeling moved across the room and enveloped Lin. The ghost's blue eyes glistened with tears. She reached her hand out towards Lin and then placed it over her heart.

When Viv said something to her cousin, Lin didn't hear her.

"Lin?" Seeing the expression on her cousin's face, Viv glanced around the room. "Is someone here?"

Lin didn't speak.

Viv placed her hand on her cousin's arm and Lin jumped.

"Do you see someone?" Viv said softly.

Lin nodded. "She's here." The cold air surrounding her was so pronounced that Lin didn't know how she kept her teeth from chattering.

"Where?" Viv questioned.

"By the piano. She's watching me."

The other people in the elegant room enjoyed the drinks and food, chatted and laughed with one another completely oblivious to the nearly see-through guest who had quietly joined them.

Feeling anxious about someone she couldn't see being nearby, Viv took a step closer to Lin. "Does she want something? Does she want your help with something?"

Lin's eyes were glued on the ghost. "I think she does."

"Do you know what it is?" Viv asked.

"I have no idea."

9

W hen the evening reception was over, Lin and Viv returned to their room, changed into pajamas, and relaxed on their beds with Viv reading a book and Lin resting against her pillow, thinking.

"Why does the ghost stay here? Why is she so sad?" Lin thought out loud.

Viv didn't look up from her book. "You'll figure it out," she mumbled.

"What's her connection to Mr. Topper and Ms. Wells?"

Viv was engrossed in her book and didn't reply.

"Is there a connection between Topper and Ms. Wells or are we forcing our theory onto the murders?" Lin asked. "Do you think there's a connection between them?"

"Mmm-hmm."

"Patricia, the innkeeper, said she thinks the ghost is from the time the factory was in business. We saw the picture of the women who worked in the factory in that old history book. One of them was my ghost. Do you think something bad happened to the ghost when she worked in the factory?"

Viv didn't answer.

"Viv? Are you listening?" Lin asked.

Closing her book, Viv placed it on her stomach. "I wasn't, no. Sorry. I thought we were relaxing."

"We can't relax. This is a working overnight stay." Lin swung her legs over the side of the bed and sighed. "Go ahead and read. I was just saying things that popped into my head. I'm going downstairs to the kitchen to get some tea. Want something?"

"No, thanks. Would you like me to come down with you?" Viv asked.

"I'll be right back." Lin put on her robe, headed down to the kitchen where several platters of cookies and a sliced chocolate cake were spread out on the large granite island. She was filling a mug with water when Patricia walked in.

"Oh, Lin. Do you have what you need? Can I get you anything else?"

With a smile, Lin looked at all the sweets and

chose a chocolate chip cookie. "I couldn't possibly want anything else."

"Is your room comfortable? Need another blanket or some more pillows?" Patricia poured a cup of coffee for herself and leaned against the counter sipping her beverage.

"Everything's great. Thank you." Lin set her mug down. "Do you know much about the building? What happened to it after the business closed? Who owned it?"

"When the business folded, the three owners sold it to a couple from town and they turned it into a rooming house. It changed hands several times, half the building was turned into the residential home and the other half was renovated into an inn."

Lin knew those details already. "Do you know anything about the people who owned the building over the years?"

"Only the people we bought the inn from. They ran it for twelve years and then they wanted to slow down, relax, travel. They were a nice couple."

"Do you know anything about Maura Wells?"

Patricia looked surprised. "I know she was a professor. She told me she was working on some research."

"Did she seem worried when she was here?" Lin asked.

"She seemed ... business-like. It was clear Ms. Wells wasn't here to chat or interact with the other guests. She was working. I didn't know the woman so I'm not sure if she was worried or not, but I would say she didn't strike me as being concerned about anything."

"Did she have any visitors?"

Patricia shook her head. "No, not that I know of."

"Did she mention meeting up with anyone? A friend? An associate?"

"She didn't bring that up. Ms. Wells went about her work quietly. She didn't engage in much conversation. She was polite and cordial, but Maura was not interested in chatter or small talk."

Lin asked, "Do you know what Maura was researching?"

"The island's economy and the economic changes that have taken place here. I think that's what she said about it."

"Was she married?"

"I don't think so."

"Did she have children?" Lin asked.

"She never mentioned having kids, but she was

pretty private. I don't know if she had any or not. She never mentioned family." Patricia's face clouded. "The police say Maura was murdered. Can you imagine? Poisoned? My husband worries that guests will think Maura was poisoned here at the inn. He hopes it doesn't scare people off."

"I wouldn't worry," Lin said. "Your reservations will probably go up. Intrigue and mystery can make a lot of people more interested in visiting a place."

"Poor woman." Patricia shook her head. "How could it have happened? Why did it happen?"

"Do you know where Maura was prior to being found in the neighbor's garden?" Lin asked.

"I don't know." Patricia wore an expression of sadness. "I wish I did. I saw her at breakfast that morning. She said she was going to the Athenaeum and to the historical museum later in the day. I don't know if she made it there or not."

"Did Maura ever tell you where she liked to have lunch or where she might have gone for coffee?"

Patricia shook her head. "She didn't."

"Did she seem friendly with any of the other guests?"

"She mostly kept to herself. She didn't really interact with anyone." The innkeeper took another swallow of her coffee. "The most we interacted was when she asked me if I could give her a tour of the building."

Lin perked up. "A tour of the building or of the inn?"

"The building."

"Did you give her a tour?"

"Yes. I can't bring anyone into the home right next door, of course, but I showed her around in here and took her down to the basement, our half of the basement."

"Why was she interested?"

"Maura knew that the building was once a factory. She asked me a lot of questions about the factory and the employees. She's an historian so it makes sense that she'd be interested."

"Can you show me the basement?" Lin asked.

Patricia's eyes widened. "Now? Do you want to go down to the basement now?"

"Can we? If it isn't an inconvenience."

"Sure. There isn't much to see ... just the building foundation. The space is pretty good sized, but it's really just an old cellar."

Patricia led Lin down the stairs into the nonde-script basement. "There's a washer and dryer down here even though we have a service take care of the linens for the inn. We have two extra refrigerators here, too. Originally, there would have been a dirt floor, but along the way, one of the owners had concrete put down. Thankfully."

"Did the factory workers work down here?" Lin asked as she walked around the basement.

"No, the factory was set up on the first floor. This area was used for some storage of extra equipment and parts. That's what I was told, anyway."

"When you brought Maura down here, did she make any comments? Did she know much about the factory that used to be here?"

"She didn't say much." Patricia shrugged. "I guess she had an interest in the silk factory since she was researching the island's economy. Shall we go back up?"

Lin nodded and thanked the innkeeper for showing her the basement. Patricia started up the stairs with Lin following, but before she took more than two steps, Lin was engulfed by cold air. Stopping, she looked across the space.

The ghost stood in the middle of the cellar staring at Lin. She wore the same light blue dress and the silver necklace around the collar. One glistening tear trailed down her cheek, and then she slowly faded away.

Sadness pulled at Lin's heart and she had to blink to keep her own tears from forming. *What happened? What made you so sad?*

"Lin?" Patricia called from the top of the stairs.

Lin swallowed hard to clear the tightness from her throat. "I'm coming." When she reached the back hall off the kitchen, Lin thanked Patricia once again and headed up to her room.

Viv opened the room's door just as Lin was about to put her key in the lock. "Where have you been? I was about to start a search party," Viv asked pulling her bathrobe around her.

Returning to their guest room, Lin told her cousin about talking to Patricia and being shown the basement.

"I'm glad I wasn't with you. Basements are creepy." Viv removed her robe and climbed under the bed covers.

"I saw the ghost down there. She was standing in the middle of the space. A tear rolled down her cheek. It made me so sad, I could barely climb back up the stairs."

Viv had her hand on her chest and a worried look on her face. "What happened to your ghost?"

"We need to figure that out. And we need to know if my ghost has some link to Maura Wells and Warren Topper." When Lin reached up and touched her horseshoe necklace, it felt slightly warm against her fingers, but she ignored the feeling since she felt chilly from the air conditioning.

"How are we going to do that?" Viv asked. "How will we figure out any of it?"

"First, we need to find out if Warren Topper was descended from one of the factory owners. Anton will have that information soon. Then we need to look through old newspapers from the time to see if an accident happened at the factory. Patricia told me that Maura Wells said she was going to the Athenaeum and to the historical museum on the afternoon she died. We should go there and ask if Maura had come in that day. If she was there, we could stop in at the cafes and restaurants in the area to see if Maura stopped in for something to eat or drink."

"Okay." Viv nodded. "Good ideas. The police probably have done that already."

"We'll ask Libby if her detective friend has shared any information with her."

With a plan set in place, they turned off the lights and the cousins prepared for sleep, but rest eluded Lin and she ended up staying awake for a long time.

The image of the ghost in the basement with a tear running down her cheek kept appearing in Lin's mind ... and it tore a mighty hole in her heart.

10

─────────

It was late afternoon by the time Lin finished with her landscaping customers. She and Nicky arrived at Anton's antique Cape-style house just as Viv was biking up to the driveway. Inside, Anton sat hunched at his old wooden kitchen table staring at his laptop with books and folders spread out over the surface.

"Come in," Anton called when he heard the rapping on the screen door off the deck.

Lin and Viv took seats at the table as the dog wagged his tail and nudged at the island historian's leg. Nicky's efforts were rewarded with a pat on the head and a scratch behind the ears.

"I've discovered some interesting information." Anton looked up at his guests. "Oh, there's a pitcher of ice water and a jug of iced tea in the fridge." He stood to get some glasses from the hutch while Viv retrieved the jugs and poured.

"What did you find?" Lin asked the man.

Anton placed a plate of cookies on the table. "Some things about Maura Wells's lineage."

Lin bit into a chocolate chip cookie and mumbled, "What is it?"

Anton shifted a large piece of paper so the young women could see better. "Ms. Wells is descended from two different natives of Nantucket."

"Two different ancestors?" Lin said with surprise.

"That's right." Anton adjusted his eyeglasses and pointed to the sheet of paper on the table. "Here. See? On her father's side, Ms. Wells was descended from Garrell Williams."

"One of the owners of the silk factory," Viv noted.

"And, see right here? On her mother's side, she was descended from a woman named Elise Porter."

"Did Williams and Elise Porter stay on Nantucket their whole lives?" Lin asked. "Is there any information on those two people?"

"Not in these databases. We'll have to look elsewhere, but we already know some things about Garrell Williams. A prominent businessman on the island, he didn't seem to suffer any lasting harm from the factory failure. He went on to form other investment groups and start other businesses. He died a very wealthy man. He lived his entire life on the island."

"Do you know if Mr. Williams had a bad reputation? Did people have bad things to say about him?" Viv asked.

"Some disagreements with associates here and there, but nothing glaring in the news accounts from back in the day," Anton said. "A few dissolved business arrangements. Nothing that particularly stands out. Nothing to indicate the man was underhanded in his dealings."

"What about Warren Topper?" Lin asked. "Was he related to one of the factory owners?"

"Mr. Topper was not descended from any of the factory owners. His ancestors were from the mainland in Massachusetts, Maine, Canada."

"So he wasn't killed as revenge for something the factory owners might have done," Viv noted. "That theory is out the window?"

"It seems the theory does not fit the evidence." Anton slid the paper with the family trees into a folder. "Libby was reluctant to give up on the idea of revenge, but she let it go after seeing Topper's family information."

"Where does that leave us then?" Lin asked.

"With the need to come up with other ideas." Anton reached for his glass of iced tea and took a swallow.

"Could Maura Wells and Warren Topper have been killed by two separate people?" Viv questioned. "Are the murders not related?"

"Unlikely," Anton said. "Two people killed in two days? Both poisoned? No, it has to be the same killer. Most murders are not committed with poison."

Lin said, "The question is ... what links Maura Wells and Warren Topper?"

"That's easy," said Viv holding a cookie. "A common enemy."

Lin crossed her arms and leaned on the table. "I guess people who don't know each other could have a common enemy. Couldn't they?"

"I suppose," Viv said slowly. "How though?"

"You could be in a grocery store, you wouldn't know most of the people who shop there, but a killer could target you and someone else because you both frequent the same market."

"In that case, there would be no personal link between the victims," Viv said. "People could get killed only because they shop in the same store. But...."

"But what?"

"There has to be a smaller thing in common in this case. Topper and Wells were on an island, they got killed a day apart, they were both poisoned. The example you gave seems too random. These two people must have some kind of connection, more than just two people who happen to be on the same island."

"Well, they don't work together," Lin said. "One is an academic and the other is an investment banker and advisor."

"So no job connection," Viv said.

"They are not the same age," Anton said. "They're fifteen years apart in age which means they couldn't have known each other in college."

"Could they be from the same town?" Lin asked.

"They did *not* grow up in the same town, nor in the same state," Anton told them.

"What about charity stuff?" Lin's eyes brightened and she made eye contact with Anton. "Libby said you two and Maura Wells often attended the same fundraising or charity events."

"However, I never saw Warren Topper at one of those events." Anton shook his head.

"Topper and Maura might have attended a fundraiser that you didn't go to," Viv pointed out.

"True, but how would they have crossed paths?"

Anton asked. "One lived in New York and one lived in Chicago."

"There *is* transportation between those two cities," Lin said with a crooked smile.

Anton raised an eyebrow. "And what? They met at an event? A person who knew them from an event decided to kill them both? Why? What outrage could have been committed at a charity event?"

Viv shrugged a shoulder. "Maybe neither one donated enough?"

Lin gave her cousin a look and ignored her comment. "I think Topper and Maura had to have known each other, and someone else had to know both of them. Something angered that someone, and he hatched a plan to kill them."

"I don't know," Anton said adjusting his glasses. "It seems too cloak and dagger."

"Why does it?" Lin asked. "Do you have a different explanation?"

"Not yet," Anton said. "But, I hope to offer an explanation after more internet sleuthing."

"How is my ghost connected to Maura Wells's and Topper's murders?" Lin asked with a questioning expression.

"Perhaps it isn't connected," Anton said.

"The ghost is a *she*, not an *it*," Lin corrected.

"She," Anton said. "Maybe the she-ghost has no connection to the murdered people."

"She does though. I can feel it." Lin ran her finger over the wooden tabletop, thinking. "She wears a necklace, the same one all the time. Every time I've seen her, she's had it on. Just like me and my necklace."

"She always has on the same blue dress, too?" Viv asked.

Lin nodded. "That's right."

"Is there anything about her appearance that gives a clue as to who she is?" Anton asked. "For example, she isn't wearing a uniform, like a nurse would. Is there anything about the way she looks or dresses that makes you know more about her?"

After a few moments pondering the question, Lin said, "I don't think so. She wears a dress typical of the times. She doesn't look poor and she doesn't look wealthy. She looks average." Lin reported to Anton what happened during her and Viv's stay at the inn. "I saw the ghost twice when we were there. She carries a heavy burden of sadness. I have to figure it out so I can help her."

"Have you seen the spirits of Maura Wells or Mr. Topper?" Anton asked.

"No, only the ghost at the inn," Lin said. "We

need to learn more about the old factory. Who worked there? Who was in charge? What were the conditions like? My ghost stays around the inn. Why does she? Something happened at that factory that keeps her there."

"We haven't found anything about an accident there," Viv said. "We've looked through those old news articles and we haven't found a word about an accident in the factory."

"Then something else happened in there. Let's go to the historical museum tomorrow. The curator or the librarian might be able to help us," Lin said. "I also think we should go back to see Mrs. Topper to ask her about charities she and her husband were involved with. Maybe she can think of another way her husband and Maura might have met."

"Okay. We have a plan," Viv said. "Tomorrow, the museum, and one day soon, we'll meet with Mrs. Topper again."

"Does Libby know the names of the men Topper met for lunch?" Lin asked.

"I can ask her," Anton said.

"We can also ask Mrs. Topper about the men when we see her." A thought flitted through Lin's brain. "Our theory about someone out for revenge on the descendants of the three factory owners has been abandoned, but the note found in Maura Wells's hand can't be dismissed. 'One down, two to go.' Then Topper was killed. So now there's one left. The killer is planning to murder one more person. What's the link? If the police don't discover the link between these people, someone else is going to die."

"*We'd* better find that link soon," Viv said.

Sitting by the screen door so he could look outside, Nicky turned his small brown head towards the three people at the kitchen table and woofed at them.

"We're trying, Nick," Lin said. "We're trying."

11

The historical museum's librarian, Felix Harper, greeted Lin and Viv when they entered the stately old building and made their way to the library section of the museum.

"Doing some research today?" Felix asked. The man was a wealth of information about Nantucket history. Tall and thin, with salt and pepper hair and blue eyes, Felix was always dressed in understated, but fashionable clothing. Today he wore well-tailored navy slacks, a crisp white shirt with a red tie, and a fitted blazer.

Lin explained what they were looking for. "We're wondering if there was ever an accident in the old silk factory in the mid 1800s."

Felix furrowed his forehead in thought. "I don't believe so. Nothing was ever reported, not during the building of the place and not while silk production was underway. No accidents of note."

Lin's shoulders sagged in disappointment.

Viv asked, "Is there any information about the people who worked at the factory?"

"I believe there is an incomplete list of factory employees dating from the early 1840s. It might take me a while to get my hands on the document." Felix looked from Viv to Lin. "This is the second time in a few days that someone has inquired about the factory and its employees."

Lin asked, "Who else asked about it? Did you know the person? Was it an island native or a tourist?"

"It was the woman who recently passed away." Felix's lips tightened in disgust. "I should say the woman who was poisoned. Nasty business," he groaned.

"Did Maura Wells say why she wanted the information?" Viv asked.

"She told me she was doing research on the island's economy," Felix said.

"Ms. Wells was descended from two island natives," Lin said. "Garrell Williams and Elise Porter."

"Williams was one of the owners of the silk factory," Felix said.

Lin nodded and told the librarian, "Mr. Williams and Ms. Porter were not related. Mr. Williams was Maura Wells ancestor on her father's side and Ms. Porter was on her mother's side."

"How interesting. She didn't mention those facts to me." Felix looked slightly put out. "If you'd like to look through what we have, I can set you up on the computers and point you to the digital newspapers from the time the factory was in operation."

"That would be great," Lin smiled.

In a few minutes time, Viv and Lin were seated in front of computers and were scrolling through the news of the day in the Nantucket papers from 1835 to 1844.

"Look for anything indicating an accident or an injury at the factory," Lin told Viv. "Or a fight or an altercation or an incident of any kind that happened there."

Two hours passed, and Viv leaned back in her chair. "I haven't found a single thing. No accidents, no nothing. No reports of trouble."

"Same for me." Lin stretched and rubbed the back of her neck. "What if we switch to reading articles about the three owners?"

"How will that help find out why your ghost remains at the inn?" Viv asked.

"I don't know. I guess it won't help." Lin rested her arms on the edge of the tabletop.

Felix walked over to the table where Viv and Lin were working. He waved a piece of paper at them. "I was able to locate the list I was looking for." He placed the paper on the table between the two young women. "These are the first twenty women who were hired to work at the silk factory, and at the bottom, it lists the owners and some of the others who had supervisory or related jobs there."

Lin thanked the man and scanned the list. Her eyes went wide when she saw one of the names. *Elise Porter.* The woman who was an ancestor of Maura Wells. "Look." Lin's voice held a tinge of excitement.

"Well, I didn't even notice that," Felix said.

"Maura Wells's great-great-great-grandmother worked at the factory?" Viv added, "I wasn't sure how many *greats* to add to the word *grandmother.*"

Lin looked across the quiet room in thought. "Maura Wells might have been researching her family line in addition to the Nantucket economy. Maybe she knew she had a relative who worked at the factory and wanted to know more about her."

"Maura was writing a book on the island

economy," Viv said. "Two of her ancestors were involved with the silk factory. That's pretty cool."

Lin clicked on the computer keyboard. "Let's look up Elise Porter on the internet." Plenty of articles mentioned a woman by that name, but none were the person they were searching for.

Felix sat down next to Lin and logged into another computer. "I'm going to access several different databases." A few minutes passed and the librarian said, "Well, this is interesting." He adjusted the screen so that Lin and Viv could see. "Here's an old article from the Nantucket newspaper dated September 3, 1843. It reports that a woman named Elise Porter went missing. Her picture is right here. This is the woman Maura Wells was descended from."

Lin almost fell off her chair. The woman in the picture was her ghost.

Felix summarized what was written in the article. "Ms. Porter had a four-year-old daughter. The woman's husband died two years before in a boat accident. A sister is quoted as saying that Elise would never have left her child and she feared foul play. A search for Ms. Porter was conducted, but she was never found."

Lin's throat had tightened so strongly she couldn't speak.

"That's awful," Viv said softly. "What could have happened to Elise?"

Lin swallowed. "What happened to the daughter?"

Felix pulled up a few other articles and read. "This one reports that after two weeks, Elise Porter still had not been found. The daughter went to the mainland to live with her aunt."

Lin made eye contact with her cousin. Now they knew her ghost's name and some of the circumstances of her life.

After thanking Felix for his help and gathering their things, Lin and Viv left the historical library and stepped out into the bright sunshine of the warm September day.

"What happened to her, Viv? What happened to my ghost?"

"She lost her life somehow," Viv said. "She was taken away from her young daughter. No wonder that ghost is wrapped in terrible sadness."

"Was it an accident? Did my ghost ... did Elise fall into the ocean and drown? Did she stumble into the marshes?" Lin paused for a moment. "Or did someone kill her?"

The young women walked along the brick side-walks through town.

"If it was an accident that took her life," Viv said, "why would Elise hang around the factory building for almost two hundred years?"

"If her life ended from an accident in the factory, there would have been a story or report in the newspaper," Lin said. A sinking feeling filled her chest. "Did someone kill her at the factory? Or near the factory?"

"And then hid her body," Viv suggested, "so she was never found."

Lin stopped and faced her cousin. "Let's go see her."

"Who?"

"Elise." Lin turned around and headed along the brick walkways for Academy Hill.

"What are you going to do?" Viv puffed as she hurried after Lin. "Barge into the inn and demand to see the ghost who lives there?"

"I'm going to stand outside and see if she shows up." Lin almost jogged along the streets to the inn.

"You don't have to run, for Pete's sake," Viv admonished her cousin. "Your ghost has been at that inn for almost two hundred years. She'll still be there if it takes us an extra five minutes to get there."

Rounding the corner near the inn, Lin came to a stop and Viv almost plowed into her.

"I'm going to wait here on the corner and see if Elise shows up. I don't want to get closer and have someone from the inn see us and wonder why we're lurking outside the place."

"Good idea." Viv was still trying to catch her breath. "I need to take up jogging."

Lin raised an eyebrow at her cousin.

"Or, maybe not." Viv wiped the back of her hand over her sweaty forehead. "Why is it still so hot? Is it ever going to cool down?"

"It's early September. It's still summer," Lin said looking down the lane towards the inn.

Twenty minutes passed and Viv asked, "How long are we going to stand here?"

Lin sighed. "I don't know."

"Maybe she doesn't know you're here," Viv suggested. "Maybe she isn't going to come."

"I guess." Lin looked dejected.

Viv said kindly, "Why don't we head to my house and make dinner. We can sit on the deck to eat and think of what to do next."

"Okay."

The young women crossed the street and started away to Viv's place when a whoosh of icy cold air surrounded Lin causing her to halt and spin around.

"What is it?" Viv whispered.

Elise Porter's spirit stood shimmering on the corner they'd just left. She stared at Lin with big eyes.

"It's Elise," Lin said softly and then took a few steps into the street to get closer to the ghost, thankful that very few cars ever drove up the lane.

Lin's heart raced as she started to speak to the ghost. "We were at the historical museum library. We found some old articles in the Nantucket newspapers."

Elise's eyes held Lin's.

"The article reported that you disappeared. There was a search, but they couldn't find you."

The atoms making up Elise's translucent body seemed to brighten.

Lin took a deep breath. "Did someone hurt you?"

Elise's body shimmered so brightly, Lin had to squint her eyes.

"Did someone kill you?" Later on, Lin would wonder if she'd actually spoken the words or if Elise had been able to hear her thoughts.

There were no tears on Elise's cheeks. Her face contorted in fury and her atoms turned bright red as if a fire raged within her. The atoms began to swirl, faster and faster, in a maniacal whirlwind. The silver necklace she wore dazzled with brilliant light and just as Lin was about to close her eyes against the painful glow, Elise's body flared crimson and the necklace exploded into a million particles, the force of it like a tornado that sent Lin falling back against the cobblestones.

"Lin." Viv shrieked as she ran to her cousin.

Blinking, Lin sat up, momentarily stunned.

Viv knelt next to her cousin and put her arm around Lin. "Did she hurt you?"

"No." Lin rubbed at her eyes. "I'm okay."

"Is she gone?" Viv looked over her shoulder.

Choked with emotion, Lin gave a slight nod as tears overflowed her lids and tumbled down her cheeks. "Someone killed her, Viv. Someone killed her."

12

I t was a busy morning at the bookstore-café with a line of people waiting to make takeout orders and almost all of the tables full with tourists and regulars. Nicky and Queenie shared the upholstered chair by the bookshelves and Lin had snagged a table when a couple finished their coffees and got up to leave. Sipping her tea and nibbling on a blueberry muffin, Lin waited for the crowd to clear so that Viv could join her for a few minutes.

The early rush lessened and Viv took a seat at Lin's table.

"Woo. Another busy morning. Early September and there's no sign of business slowing." Viv leaned forward so people sitting at the nearest tables wouldn't hear her comments. "The employees didn't recognize Warren Topper when I showed them his pictures on the internet. I don't recall seeing the man in here. Mrs. Topper said this was his favorite café. Really? I don't know how that could be true if none of us recognize him."

"I know all of you work hard to remember the customers," Lin said. "You make people feel welcome. If nobody recalls seeing Topper, he couldn't have been in here very often, and certainly not on a regular basis."

Viv took a piece of Lin's muffin. "Does Mrs. Topper know what she's talking about? Maybe she confused my place with another café. When she said her husband might have come to the café right before he met his friends for lunch, a flash of nervousness raced through me. Even though she didn't come out and say it, I felt like she blamed my bookstore for poisoning her husband."

Lin kept her voice low. "Maybe Mr. Topper lied to his wife about his favorite café. Maybe he told her he was going to the bookstore when he was actually going elsewhere."

"Huh." Viv's blue eyes flashed. "What was he up to? We need to have another chat with Maggie Topper."

"I called her. We're meeting late this afternoon when we both finish up at work."

"Good." Viv sipped from Lin's teacup. "How are we going to help Elise leave the inn and cross over?"

Lin sighed. "I guess the question is what does she need before she's ready to cross. If we figure out who killed her, it's impossible to bring him to justice. He's long dead. That can't be what she needs."

"Maybe it is what she needs. Maybe she wants her killer named." Viv glanced around at the other tables to be sure no one was listening to their conversation. "Her body was never found. If we find it, maybe she'll be free to move on. Elise is the one we need to focus on, not Maura Wells's or Warren Topper's murders."

Lin ran her index finger over the smooth porcelain of her teacup. "I have a feeling they might be connected to Elise in some way."

Viv's eyebrows shot up. "The murders have happened nearly two hundred years apart. How can there be a connection?"

With a frown, Lin shrugged. "I don't know."

Viv leaned against her chair back. "Okay. We'll keep going with all three murders. Have you talked to Libby? Do the police have any suspects?"

"They aren't saying."

Viv gave a half-smile. "I'll meet you at your house

later this afternoon and we'll go see Mrs. Topper.
And after that meeting, we'll figure out what's next."

THE TWO COUSINS rang the bell and Maggie Topper
opened the door to greet them, led them through the
house and out to the back porch overlooking the
beautifully landscaped yard. When they were seated
in the comfortable chairs, Viv started the
conversation.

"I spoke with my employees at the bookstore and
none of them recognized your husband. Is it
possible that he confused the name of the café he
liked to visit?"

Maggie looked at Viv with a neutral expression.
"Perhaps your employees are mistaken. Viv's Victus.
That's the name of your store, right?"

"It is," Viv nodded.

"That's where Warren liked the coffee."

Viv realized it wasn't worth pressing the issue.
"Could you tell us the names of your husband's
friends? The two men he met for lunch that day."

"Paul Monroe and Lenny Page. They both have
summer homes on the island."

"Are they from New York City?" Lin asked.

"Yes, they are."

"You mentioned when we were here last time that you had gone to a friend's home before your husband left for his lunch meeting," Lin reminded the woman. "Who did you visit?"

"Rosalind McKenna. She lives near Miacomet beach."

Maggie seemed to be getting tense so Lin asked her about her property. "Your home is lovely. You told us it's been in the family for many years?"

"Yes, it has. Nearly two hundred years. It's been handed down from generation to generation. We treasure the place."

"You have a lot of land?" Lin asked.

"Five acres. It was larger initially. When my ancestor built the home, it had fifteen acres, but some of the acreage was sold off over the years. I intend to keep it as is. No more selling off any land ... unless, of course, the price is right."

The doorbell rang and Maggie told her guests that the housekeeper would answer it. In a few minutes, a tall, good-looking man in his mid-fifties with light brown hair and brown eyes came out of the house to the porch and Maggie rose to greet him.

"Paul." The two hugged and then she turned to make introductions.

"This is Paul Monroe. He was a close friend of Warren's ... and of mine."

The man took a seat. "I came by to see how you're doing," he told Maggie.

"As well as can be expected." Maggie pushed at her bangs.

Paul addressed Lin and Viv. "You help out the police?"

Lin nodded and then fibbed, "Only on an as-needed basis. The department is often short-handed and we do some research for them when time allows."

"Can you tell us what happened when Warren arrived to meet you for lunch?" Viv asked.

Paul shook his head and ran his hand through his hair. "What a day. It still seems surreal." After taking in a deep breath, he said, "Warren arrived. Lenny Page and I were already at the bar waiting for him. He ordered a gin and tonic. The three of us talked. Warren's face became flushed. He was sweating. I thought it was a reaction to the alcohol. We went on conversing, but then Warren began to seem unsteady, he started to sway a little." Paul looked over to Maggie. "Would you rather we discuss this inside?"

Maggie had her hand at her throat. "No. I'm okay. Go ahead."

"I asked Warren if he wasn't feeling well. He didn't respond. He started to tug at his collar. Even though his cheeks were red, his face grew pale. Some spittle formed at the corners of his mouth." Paul shifted in his seat. "Warren's eyes rolled back in his head and then he ... Warren collapsed."

"He was unconscious?" Lin asked.

"He certainly seemed to be. While Lenny called '911', I knelt beside Warren and spoke his name, but he didn't seem to be awake. Restaurant employees rushed over to help. There wasn't anything to be done. It was a terrible, terrible day."

"Had Warren been concerned about anything lately?" Viv asked.

"No. He seemed his usual self," Paul said.

"Was he angry about anything?"

Paul sat back in his chair. "He didn't express any anger when we were together."

"So he wasn't afraid or worried?" Lin asked.

"Not when he was with me." Paul shook his head.

"Any financial concerns?"

Paul looked surprised. "No."

"Was he experiencing any trouble at his office?" Viv asked. "With an employee? A client?"

"Warren never mentioned anything of the sort, at least nothing of importance. We all have some minor issues at our firms from time to time. It was just business as usual."

"Do you know if Warren stopped somewhere before he came to meet you?" Lin questioned.

"I don't know if he did or not," Paul said.

"Did Warren have a friend or acquaintance in town that he might have stopped to see?"

"In town? I don't believe so."

"He didn't mention having to stop somewhere before meeting with you?" Lin asked.

Paul rubbed the side of his face. "I don't recall if he said anything like that."

"How long have you known Warren?"

"Since we were in our mid-twenties. We went to law school together. His career path led him into investments and finance. I joined a law firm."

"Was he comfortable in his position?" Lin questioned. "Did he want to continue working for some time?"

"Warren loved his work. He traveled a good deal, but he was used to it."

"Where did he have to travel to?" Viv asked.

"Not far. Boston, Atlanta, Chicago, D.C."

Lin directed her question to Maggie. "He traveled often?"

"Every other week or so. He'd be gone from two to five days." Maggie stood up. "Excuse me for a minute. I need to go into the house for a moment."

When she was gone, Paul said, "I don't know how Maggie is handling this nightmare."

Lin said, "I'm sorry to ask this, but we need to cover all the bases. Was Warren faithful to Maggie? Was there any trouble between them?"

Paul's face took on a look of concern. "I ... I don't know their private details. Warren didn't confide such things to me."

"If there was another woman, would Warren have talked to you about it?" Viv questioned.

"I'm not sure." Paul's eyes moved uncomfortably around the porch.

"If he and Maggie were having any marital or financial struggles, would Warren have talked to you about that?" Lin asked.

Paul said, "Warren never brought up anything like that so I'll assume everything was fine between them. Financially, there were no troubles. Maggie inherited wealth and then increased it. Believe me, there are no money worries in this family."

Maggie came back outside and sat down. "We're having a memorial service for Warren and a luncheon here in two weeks. There will be two tents, one for the service and one for the sit-down lunch." The woman rubbed her eyes and looked around the yard. "I need to get someone to do some landscaping back here. I want everything to be prefect for Warren."

Paul glanced over at Lin and then said to Maggie, "You have the owner of the best landscaping company on the island right here on your porch. Ask her to do it."

"Oh, that's right." Maggie made eye contact with Lin. "Could your company handle it? On such short notice?"

"I think we might be able to," Lin said. "My partner and I could come back to talk to you about what you hope to have done for the service and then make a decision if we can fit it in." As soon as the words were out of Lin's mouth, a shiver of unease washed over her skin.

"That would be wonderful, "Maggie said. "I'd be forever grateful."

Lin looked out over the expansive rear yard and something about it made her heart sink.

13

"I felt dread when Maggie Topper asked if Leonard and I would landscape the backyard before the memorial service for Warren is held there," Lin said as she prepared the mushroom and onion appetizers.

"Why dread?" Viv sat at the kitchen island sprinkling shredded cheese over the tops of the mini quiche. "Maggie Topper is loaded. Why not take the job and put some extra money in your bank account?"

"We'll listen to what she wants and if it's reasonable to manage it in two weeks, we'll do it, but there's something about being on that property and knowing the husband was poisoned, it just gives me the creeps."

"Charge her extra then ... for your pain and suffering." Viv sipped from her wine glass.

"Yeah, maybe." Lin absent-mindedly reached up and rubbed her thumb over her horseshoe necklace.

"You know what?" Viv said noticing her cousin's finger touching the necklace. "Your cottage's layout is similar to your necklace."

Lin cocked her head. "What do you mean?"

"You're wearing a horseshoe necklace. Your house is designed in a horseshoe shape ... a U-shape with the deck in the middle of the U."

"I never thought of that."

Lin's house had a master bedroom and bath located at one side of a U, a small guest bedroom and the living room were at the base of the U, and the kitchen and dining room were located on the other side of the U. The deck was in the middle, accessible from the master bedroom, the living room, and the kitchen.

Nicky and Queenie were outside on the deck resting in the cushioned Adirondack chairs.

"It's a coincidence, isn't it," Lin said looking out at the two snoozing animals.

"Is it?" One of Viv's eyebrows was raised in question.

"No one designed the house to resemble a horseshoe," Lin smiled. "It just fit the lot well and gave each small wing of the house a door to the outside."

"How can you be sure it wasn't created this way on purpose to reflect that necklace of yours?"

Lin only chuckled and returned to work on the rest of the appetizers.

When Viv finished the quiches, she picked up Lin's laptop and began to tap at the keys. "I'm curious. I'm looking up Maggie Topper. I want to know how much she's worth."

"Why?"

"She gives the impression of wealth and privilege. I want to know if she's putting that on or if she really came from a background of advantage. Also, I'm just plain nosy."

After a minute of silence, Viv let out a loud whistle and Lin jumped.

"What?"

"Listen to this. Maggie Topper is worth ... get ready ... a billion dollars."

"No way." Lin walked over to where her cousin was sitting and looked over her shoulder at the laptop screen.

"Yup. That's what it says, estimated worth, one billion." Viv nudged Lin with her elbow. "You better double your price for her landscaping job."

"How did she make the money?"

"She inherited a whole kit and caboodle of it, but she made smart investments herself." Viv read off the list of successful business investments Maggie had made with her money.

"Yikes," was all Lin could say.

"She's a smart cookie," Viv said. "Although, if I inherited a half billion dollars, I bet I could do something with it to make it increase."

"If only...." Lin smiled and patted her cousin's shoulder.

Viv kept reading about the woman. "Her father, grandfather, and great-grandfather ran the investment company she inherited. Her mother was a lawyer, her grandmother was a physician, and her great-grandmother was a scientist. What a family."

"A bunch of over-achievers."

Viv said, "I wonder if all that wealth and history of achievement made Warren feel self-conscious or less important. It seems he didn't come from money."

Lin popped the mushroom turnovers into the oven.

Viv went on, "The article mentions Maggie's Nantucket ancestor. His name was Vernon Willard."

Lin spun around when she heard the name. "Willard? Where did I hear that name before?"

"Maggie introduced herself to us as Maggie Willard Topper," Viv reminded Lin.

"That wasn't it." Lin tried to remember where she'd heard it previously.

"He was an important and successful business-man," Viv read from the online article. "He made tons of money. He bought land and had the house built on upper Main Street that now belongs to Maggie. He had a reputation of being unscrupulous and devious in his dealings." Viv looked up. "Sheesh. Is that how every rich person makes their money? By cheating and grubbing?"

"I'll let you know after I make my first million," Lin joked. "So Vernon Willard was the start of the Willard fortune. Vernon Willard. I've heard that name before now."

Where she saw the name suddenly jumped into her mind. "I remember now. His name was listed as an employee of the silk factory. It was printed on the sheet of paper Felix gave us at the library."

"Vernon Willard worked at the factory? I wonder if Maggie knows that fact," Viv said.

"Can you find any more information on Vernon?" Lin asked.

Viv queried the man's name and quite a few articles appeared on the screen. "Here's some information. Vernon was a financial officer and accountant at the silk factory. It doesn't give details, but this article says that the three owners had a falling out with Vernon and those differences of opinion, along with the failing mulberry trees, led to a fraying of the relationships as tensions mounted over the business problems. It seems there was a parting of the ways, and not a friendly one." Viv read on. "Vernon bought and sold many businesses over the course of his lifetime. He invested well. He made a sizable fortune." Viv looked up. "Too bad ole Vernon wasn't an ancestor of ours. Lucky Maggie ... Vernon started the fortune almost two hundred years ago and Maggie inherited it."

Lin leaned against the kitchen counter. "I don't know why what you just said made me think of this, but something's been picking at me since we were at Maggie's house."

"What's bothering you?"

"Something felt off to me when the friend, Paul Monroe, came out to the porch. The relationship between Paul and Maggie seemed slightly strained to me. Maybe it's their shared grief that made them seem awkward with one another. I don't know. I feel like there's something there that could be meaningful."

"Meaningful, how?" Viv's eyes widened. "Oh. Do you think they might be having an affair?"

"I'm not sure that's it. I sort of felt like Paul knows something he isn't sharing."

Viv leaned forward. "Could Paul be the one who poisoned Warren Topper?"

"I think what you said about Vernon Willard having a falling out with the three silk factory workers made me think of this. Were Paul and Warren close to having a falling out? Was Paul angry with Warren over something?"

Nicky and Queenie came in from the deck and sat on the kitchen floor listening to the conversation.

"Do you think Maggie knows anything about trouble between her husband and Paul?" Viv asked.

"I wouldn't think so, but maybe she suspects something?"

"This is interesting. I didn't pick up on any of this when we were there."

"I'm not sure what's going on," Lin said. "But I feel there's something that bears looking into, either at Paul's and Maggie's relationship or whether Paul knows something important he isn't talking about, or if Paul's and Warren's friendship was fraying, and if it was, why was it?"

Nicky let out a woof.

"Nick agrees with you." Viv reached down and scratched the dog's ears. "And so do I." Standing up, she walked over to the stove. "Now let's get those appetizers out of the oven and go change. John and Jeff will be here any minute."

Lin put on an oven mitt and removed the cookie sheets of quiches, turnovers, and mini pizzas. The four young people were planning to meet for drinks and appetizers before heading into town to attend a restaurant party where a well-known singer who was a native of the island would be performing.

Lin was looking forward to the evening to have a break from thinking about her ghost and the murders of Warren Topper and Maura Wells, and when she heard Jeff knock on the screen door and come into the house, her heart skipped a beat.

When John arrived full of excitement over a house deal he'd just closed on, everyone headed out to the deck, lit the candles, poured drinks, and enjoyed the appetizers while Viv's boyfriend told them the details about the sale he made only a few hours ago.

The friends chatted and laughed and relaxed

together until it was time to head to the party. They cleared the deck table and loaded the dishwasher and got ready to leave the house.

Jeff wrapped Lin his arms and kissed her. "Thanks for the drinks and appetizers."

When they stepped out of the hug, Lin's horseshoe necklace caught on Jeff's sweater and she had to grab at it to prevent it from breaking.

"We've been permanently hitched together," Jeff kidded. He carefully unhooked the piece of jewelry and then took Lin's hand as they followed Viv and John out of the house.

With her thumb and index finger holding the small white-gold horseshoe hanging from her necklace, Lin remembered how Elise's own necklace had exploded into a million pieces the last time she'd seen the ghost.

Lin didn't know why, but thinking about what had happened to the ghost's silver chain caused an icy shiver to run down her back.

14

The bar-restaurant was located down at the docks overlooking the harbor and boats. An outside patio with tables and chairs and several seating groups clustered around glass coffee tables bustled with people enjoying appetizers and drinks. The band played inside, but speakers brought the music out to the patrons on the patio.

Warm temperatures without a bit of humidity and a clear sky full of stars enhanced the crowd's enjoyment as people chatted and mingled.

"What a great night," Viv smiled taking in the scene.

Jeff managed to find a table on the patio when a group vacated the spot.

"Perfect," John said as he scanned the fashion-ably dressed people. "This is going to be fun."

The foursome ordered drinks and light dinners.

"I think everyone on the island is here," Lin chuckled. "I didn't think this place would be so crowded."

"The band is popular," Viv pointed out. "They've got two songs getting a lot of airplay. It's great to see them so successful."

When they'd finished their meals, two women came over to the table to chat with Viv and Lin, and Jeff and John wandered off to the other side of the patio to talk with some acquaintances.

When their girlfriends went inside to see the band, Lin and Viv sat listening to the music until a man's voice greeted them. Paul Monroe, wearing tan chinos and a navy blazer, sat down at the table with the cousins. His eyelids looked heavy and his speech was slightly slurred from a couple of drinks too many.

"How are you doing?" Viv asked.

"I'm keeping busy and drinking too much to avoid thinking about Warren's murder."

"Are you here alone?" Lin asked.

Paul nodded. "My wife went back to the main-land for a few meetings. I didn't want to sit at home alone sulking so I decided to come down in the hopes I'd run into some friends."

"How is Mrs. Topper doing?" Viv asked.

"She's holding together fairly well. Of course, it might be a different story when she's alone."

"You said you and Warren were friends for almost thirty years?" Lin questioned.

"That's right." Paul lifted his drink to his lips, saw that the glass was empty, set it down, and flagged a waiter for another. "Time flies."

"You know Maggie pretty well?"

"Sure. Well, not as well as I knew Warren, but my wife and I have been friends with the Toppers for years. We did things as couples, golfed, went to the beach, met other friends for dinner and drinks."

"You never noticed a crack in the Toppers' marriage?" Viv asked.

"No." Paul seemed about to say more, but hesitated.

"Was there ever disharmony between Warren and Maggie?"

When the waiter returned with a fresh drink for Paul, he picked it up and took a long swallow. "Maybe there was some friction from time to time."

"How do you mean?"

"Maggie isn't the easiest person to get

along with."

Lin and Viv waited to see if Paul would say more.

Paul slouched and rested an elbow on the table. "Maggie's nice and all, but she's got some attitude. The woman is loaded. She inherited a bundle. She liked to lord it over Warren sometimes."

"Warren did well though, didn't he?" Lin leaned forward.

"Sure, he did, but it was no match for millions and millions of inherited wealth. Maggie is smart. She grew her business and expanded the fortune. She enjoyed rubbing it in Warren's face."

"How did Warren take that?"

"Usually fine. Sometimes they'd have words though. Things could be tense between them." Paul looked out over the dark harbor, the lights of the boats shimmering off the water. "From the outside, Warren's and Maggie's lives looked perfect. Looks can be deceiving."

"Would they have divorced?" Viv asked.

"I certainly don't think so. Maggie and Warren had their place in society. They preferred to keep up appearances."

Lin looked Paul in the eyes. "Does Maggie confide in you?"

Paul shook his head. "No. The friendship isn't

like that. Maggie doesn't even confide in my wife." The man's lip curled. "Actually, I can't see Maggie doing that with anyone. She's a formidable presence and likes it that way. She would never show weakness. She would never show that she needed someone else."

"That's kind of sad." Viv frowned.

"I suppose it is," Paul said. "I never thought of it that way."

Lin asked, "Do you remember anything from the afternoon Warren died? Anything that seemed inconsequential at the time, but now might seem odd or unusual?"

Paul's eyes were bloodshot. "I don't think so."

"Did the bartender take too long to make Warren's drink? Did he seem to keep his hand over it in an odd way? Did he give it to someone else by mistake and then deliver it to Warren?"

Paul shook his head slowly and said in a soft voice. "I didn't notice anything like that."

John caught Viv's eye from across the patio and gestured towards Paul sitting with them, and she gave her boyfriend a reassuring smile and a wave.

Paul noticed and asked, "Am I keeping you? Do you need to meet someone?"

"Not at all. It's my boyfriend. He's chatting with

some friends he hasn't seen in a while," Viv told the man.

"I'm going to miss Warren. I always enjoyed his company. I didn't realize how much until this happened." Paul rubbed the back of his hand over his eyes. "Listen. Something's been nagging at me for a couple of days."

Lin's nervous system began to buzz. "Oh?"

"Yeah. It's probably nothing, but...."

"What is it?" Viv asked with a raised eyebrow.

"I wasn't quite up front with you when I saw you at Maggie's place." Paul kept his gaze on his drink. "I didn't feel comfortable talking to you with Maggie nearby. When she went inside and left the three of us sitting on the porch, I didn't know how much time we had before she would come back out."

Lin wished Paul would get to the point.

Paul glanced around the patio and looked over his shoulders. "It's been bothering me." He swallowed hard. "Warren was seeing a woman."

With her heart in her throat, Lin tried to keep her voice even when she asked, "Was he?"

Paul gave a curt nod. "On one hand, I feel like I'm betraying Warren by bringing this up, but on the other hand, I'm concerned and feel I should share."

"Okay." Lin wanted to grab Paul by the shoulders and shake the words out of him.

"Warren had been seeing this woman for a long time. A couple of years. She lives in Boston. She's a real estate attorney. Warren met her at a charity event and they hit it off."

"Maggie has no inkling of this?" Viv asked.

"If she did, she'd have killed Warren." Paul's eyes widened at what he'd said. "Not literally. I mean she would have been furious. I think she would have kicked Warren out."

"How did Warren keep this secret for so long?" Lin questioned.

Paul shrugged. "The woman is in Boston. Warren went there frequently for business."

"Warren told you about her?"

Paul rested his forehead in his hand. "I wish he hadn't. It makes me feel terrible. I wasn't thrilled when he told me and we had a few words over it, but I just thought it's his decision and it's his life. It wasn't my place to judge."

"Why are you telling us about this now?" Lin asked.

Paul kept his eyes on his drink. "I'm worried about something. Not only did Warren keep his affair a secret from Maggie, but he kept the fact he was married from this woman."

"She didn't know Warren was married?" Viv's eyes bugged out.

Paul shook his head.

"Why are you worried?"

"What if the woman found out about Maggie? What if the woman found out Warren was married?"

Lin sat up straight. "Wait. You think the woman from Boston might have found out Warren had lied to her for two years? You think she might have come to Nantucket?"

Paul raised his head and looked Lin in the eyes. "Do you think it's possible? Do you think she might have killed Warren?"

"Gosh." Viv's hand went to her throat.

"Do you know the woman's name?" Lin asked.

Paul hesitated.

"You *do* know her name?"

"Yes."

"Why are you telling *us* about this affair of Warren's?" Viv asked.

"You're doing research for the police, aren't you?"

Lin gave a quick nod.

140

"I thought I should tell you about this ... just in case."

"I think you should go to the police and tell them what you just shared with us," Lin suggested.

Paul's face took on a frightened expression. "No way. You tell them, just leave my name out of it. I'm not going to the police station. Someone will see me and want to know why I went there."

"Call the police and ask them to come to your home," Lin said.

Paul's eyes flashed. "Absolutely not. My wife will want to know what I'm talking with them about. She'll want the details. She'd never forgive me for hiding Warren's secret for so long. No. It's not an option. And if you tell the police it was me who spoke with you, I'll deny it."

Lin spoke gently. "Can you tell us the woman's name? Do you know her name?"

Paul bit his lip. "I swear I'll deny everything if you tell the police I shared this information with you."

"We won't mention your name to the police," Lin promised.

Shifting his eyes around nervously, Paul sighed. "Sofia Ricci."

"She's an attorney? Do you know where she works?"

"Ricci, Johnson, and Freedman." Paul looked deflated, but then he stood up suddenly. "Excuse me," he mumbled. "I'm going to the restroom to be sick."

Viv made eye contact with her cousin. "How about you and me take a quick trip to Boston one of these days?"

With anxiety gripping her stomach, Lin said, "Unfortunately, I think that might be a very good idea."

15

Leonard sat in the passenger seat of Lin's truck with his arms around Nicky. The little dog was standing on the man's lap so he could see out the window as Lin drove to Maggie Topper's house.

"Then Paul told us that Warren was having an affair with a woman who lives in Boston. The affair had been going on for two years and she had no idea Warren was married. And listen to this ... Paul is afraid the woman found out that Warren had lied about not being married and she came here and poisoned him."

Leonard turned quickly towards Lin. "Seriously? What a mess. How did Topper keep his affair from his wife? How did he keep the fact he had a wife secret from the woman?"

"I guess Warren traveled quite a bit for his work. He frequently went to Boston and Chicago. He was gone for most of the week and he traveled about two weeks out of each month."

"That guy was a real jerk." Leonard ran his hand over the dog's fur. "What a rat. Did you pass the information along to the police?"

"We told Libby about it, but we kept Paul Monroe's name out of it. She'll share the information with her detective friend."

Lin turned the wheel and steered the truck down the Toppers' long driveway. "Maggie Topper is super wealthy. She knows what she wants. She likes the best. Keep that in mind when we're deciding to take this job or not. We might not want to deal with her if she's going to be a royal pain about everything we do."

"Good to know."

The truck came to a stop, but before they got out, Lin asked about Leonard's ghost-wife, Marguerite.

"Have you seen Marguerite lately?"

"I see her every day, Coffin."

"I wasn't sure. Did you ask her about my ghost? Did you ask her about Elise?"

Leonard ran his fingers over the scruff of beard on

his chin. "I brought it up. I could tell by Marguerite's face that she didn't seem to know anything about Maura Wells's or Topper's deaths. I asked about Elise. Marguerite just stared at me and then she lifted her hand to her throat, like she was touching a necklace."

Lin's mouth dropped open. "A necklace?" She told Leonard how when she asked Elise if someone had killed her, her atoms flamed red and her necklace exploded into a million pieces. "Do you think Marguerite knows Elise wears the same necklace all the time?"

Leonard's eyes were glued to Lin's face. "You think because Marguerite touched her collar bone, it relates to Elise wearing a necklace?"

"It could, couldn't it?"

"I have no idea. You're the one who figures this stuff out." Leonard held the dog, opened the truck door, stepped out, and placed Nicky on the ground just as Maggie Topper opened the front door to meet them.

"You brought a dog?" Maggie's nose turned up and Nicky gave her a dirty look.

"He's well-trained and obedient," Leonard said. "He won't be an issue."

After introductions were made, the woman led

the landscapers to the rear yard, still giving the little brown dog a nasty expression.

"You have a beautiful property," Leonard complimented the space. "It's walking distance to town, but private and secluded."

"It's been in my family for nearly two hundred years." Maggie's posture was straight. She was clearly proud of her home.

"It must have started with more land?" Leonard asked.

"Today the property consists of five acres. Initially there was much more land, but it was sold off over the years. I'm resistant to selling any more, but I've had an offer for two acres that is difficult to resist."

Leonard asked which two acres were involved in the request to purchase.

Maggie pointed to the left rear of the property. "It would take a good part of the trees over there. A buffer of the woods would remain. I don't know. My ancestor who purchased the land and had the house built was adamant that these three acres must stay with the house." Maggie shrugged. "Some quirk of his that certain acreage couldn't be sold off." She chuckled. "I suppose I don't wish to tempt his wrath should I want to sell off some land so I'll be sure to keep the necessary three acres."

Maggie walked Lin and Leonard around the backyard explaining where the two tents would be set up for the memorial service and what she wanted the yard to look like.

"Is it possible to do the work in time for the service?" she asked.

"It's possible to do the work," Lin said. "The question is ... can we fit this project in while maintaining our regular workload."

"When will you decide?" Maggie looked impatient. "I'll be happy to pay more because of the time crunch. Why don't I go inside and get some cool drinks and you two can have a private discussion about it?"

When Maggie had disappeared into the house, Lin asked, "What do you think?"

"Mrs. Topper is no worse that some of our other clients."

"Do we want another difficult client?" Lin asked.

"Well, one good thing is it's a temporary job." Leonard glanced around the yard thinking over the amount of work the project would entail. "We wouldn't have to put up with her for long."

Lin took a step closer to Leonard. "Something

about Maggie makes me uncomfortable. She doesn't seem too broken up over losing her husband."

"Maybe it's a relief to be rid of him. From what Paul Monroe told you, Maggie was pretty haughty about her money and her status. Maybe she's glad to be free to find someone new who's more on her level of wealth."

"That seems really harsh." Lin scowled.

"The world is harsh, Coffin. You gotta surround yourself with the right people, people who care, people with kind hearts. It doesn't matter how much money someone has. That's not what's important."

Lin smiled at her partner. "Someone recently reminded me of that ... and about the things that really matter." She was referring to what Leonard said to her on her birthday when he gave her Marguerite's sailor's valentine, that only two things matter in life ... love and friendship.

Leonard winked. "And don't forget it."

Nicky, sitting on the grass next to Lin and Leonard, let out a long whine.

"Hold your horses, young Fido," Leonard said to the dog. "We're almost done here."

"What should we do about the job?"

"It would be a lot of money," Leonard pointed out. "For a short burst of work."

Lin narrowed her eyes and kidded her partner. "I thought money didn't matter."

"We need to eat, Coffin."

"What do you think we should charge for the project?"

When Leonard told her the suggested price, Lin asked, "Are you inflating the price because Maggie is rich?"

"It's a case of supply and demand. She wants us to do the job. We have limited time and most of it is taken up with our regular clients. She's in a rush. I've taken those factors into account and came up with a price that is fair to all parties."

"Maybe you should have been a lawyer," Lin said.

"That would drive me nuts. I like being outside."

Nicky whined again.

"What's wrong with you, Nick?" As soon as she asked the question, a cold sweep of air surrounded Lin and she turned slightly in the direction the wind blew.

Elise Porter's translucent form stood off to the side of the yard, her eyes pinned on Lin.

Leonard took one look at Lin's face and asked, "What's wrong with *you*?"

"Elise is here," Lin whispered.

"What does she want?"

"I don't know."

Nicky thumped his little tail on the grass and stared in Elise's direction. The ghost-woman didn't move, she just kept looking at Lin. The sadness coming from her was almost suffocating.

"I'm trying to figure it all out," Lin said softly to the ghost. "I haven't forgotten you."

Elise's atoms grew brighter and began to swirl. Faster and faster they went until the spirit's form blurred, then flared, and was gone.

"Did she leave?" Leonard asked.

"Yes, she's gone."

"Did she say anything?"

"They never speak to me."

"They don't make it easy, do they?"

"They certainly don't." Lin sighed feeling the pull of sadness even though the ghost was gone.

"You okay?" Leonard asked.

Lin nodded. "Yeah."

"Shall we go see what's keeping Mrs. Topper?"

The landscaping partners turned towards the back terrace of the house when they saw Maggie coming out with a tray of glasses. The woman set it down on the porch table and waved them over.

They'd only gone a few steps when Lin stopped and reached for her horseshoe necklace.

"Elise wasn't wearing her necklace. She didn't have her silver chain on."

Leonard gave Lin a questioning look.

"Every time I've seen her she's been wearing that necklace." Lin glanced around at the lush green lawn, the tall trees, the flowering hydrangeas.

"You told me it exploded the last time you were with her," Leonard said.

"Yes, but...."

"But, what?"

"She should have it on. She's supposed to have it on. The necklace breaking apart was only a ... it was a symbol of something." Lin rubbed her forehead. "It was trying to tell me something."

"Do you have some idea what the message might be?" Leonard asked.

Looking back to where Elise had been standing, Lin shook her head, slowly and sadly, from side to side.

16

While Lin worked on the flower beds edged around the wide porch of the Mystic Inn, Nicky rested in the grass beside her. A few of the inn's guests were sitting in white rocking chairs admiring the view of the patio, gardens, and green lawn. Kneeling beside one of the gardens, Lin could hear a woman's voice coming from the porch speaking into a phone.

"I saw them. I couldn't make out everything they were saying, but they were arguing. It was them. No, I'm not mistaken." The woman cursed. "I am not exaggerating. It was those two people who got poisoned."

Lin almost dropped her trowel and she leaned back on her heels to peer up to the porch. The woman who was talking into the phone had dark brown hair cut short around her face and appeared to be in her mid-forties.

"I'm going for a walk now," the woman said and ended the call.

When the woman started down the steps to the lawn, Lin scrambled to her feet.

"Excuse me," Lin said.

The brown-haired woman turned. "Yes?"

Lin introduced herself. "I do the landscaping here at the inn. I was working on those beds near the porch and I overheard your conversation. You heard the two people who were poisoned arguing with one another?"

The brown-haired woman stepped closer with a look of appreciation that someone was interested in her experience, and might like to gossip. "I did. It was definitely them."

"Maura Wells and Warren Topper?"

"Yes. I couldn't remember their full names. It was them and they were having an argument." The woman extended her hand. "Penny Millbury."

"I live year round on the island," Lin said. "Mr. Topper lived here in the summers. It's a close knit community. We were shocked by the murders. Where did you see Maura and Warren?"

"They were in that playground down near Brant

Point. You know it? It was the night before the woman was found dead. It was dark. I was restless so I went for a walk. I sat down on a bench overlooking the harbor. There was tall seagrass separating me from the playground."

"You heard their voices?"

"Yes. They were having a heated conversation. I thought it was some marital spat going on between them. Maybe they'd been out for dinner and drinks and an argument started and escalated," Penny said. "I tried to ignore them."

"What happened?"

"I couldn't make out every word they were saying, but I heard enough to stand up and take a look at them."

"Did they see you?"

"If they did, they didn't pay any attention to me."

"What were you able to hear?" Lin asked.

"The woman was saying things like *I don't know how you could do that ... you deserve to be found out ... you deserve to be disgraced.* It sounded like a professional breach of some kind. I thought maybe she was his boss and he'd done something illegal at work."

"Did she say anything else that might have given you a clue to what the man had done?"

"Not really. He was going on like some pathetic

pansy. He asked her not to turn him in, or something like that. He promised to change his ways and do things right from now on. He knew he'd done the wrong thing, but I bet he admitted that only because he got caught. I bet he stole money from the company and got caught red-handed. Then he went boo-hoo about it … and promised he'd never do it again. Sure, he won't."

"How did the woman take it?"

"She said something like … *there is no letting this go*. She wasn't having any of it. She whirled around and walked away, fast. I should have applauded. I bet he stole from the company, that woman found out what he did and confronted him, and he panicked about losing his job and his income … and decided to kill her."

"If he killed her, then who killed him?" Lin asked.

"Maybe someone out to avenge the woman?" Penny said. "I almost died when I saw their pictures on the news."

"Did you tell the police you saw them arguing?"

"No. What for? They must know the guy did something wrong. It was probably easy to find out. They must know he killed the woman."

"Maybe you should tell the police what you overheard," Lin suggested.

"I don't want to get involved. No, I don't. I didn't see him kill her or anything."

"What you overheard might be helpful."

"I don't see how," Penny said. "The police can get the information they need from the firm those two worked at. I'm sure people at the company must have suspected his wrongdoing."

"I don't think Maura Wells and Warren Topper worked at the same place," Lin said.

"No? Well, they must have *some* kind of business interaction. Maybe they're both involved with a certain charity and she found out he was stealing from them. It could be a lot of things. But it was absolutely clear that he did something wrong, she discovered his shenanigans, and was going to report him. My guess is he didn't care to be revealed so he killed her."

"Did the man seem threatening when they were having their argument?" Lin asked.

"I tried to keep my eyes looking away from them, but my impression was that he wasn't about to strike the woman and he didn't try to hurt her. The idea to get rid of her must have been hatched later that night." Penny gave a confidant nod.

Several couples strolled along the brick walkways of the inn's property past the two women.

Lin asked, "You're pretty sure the woman you saw that night was the person who got killed the next day?"

"I'm positive it was the woman who got murdered." Penny nodded for emphasis.

"It was dark out, right?" Lin asked. "You were able to see their faces clearly?"

"They were standing under a streetlamp. The light reflected off their faces. I'm sure it was her ... and I'm sure it was him."

"Had you ever seen them before that night?" Lin asked.

"Never."

"I can see that the man might have been so upset that he came up with the plan to kill Maura, but it seems he had to plot it out quickly since the attack came the very next afternoon," Lin said. "Do you think he had enough time to make a plan to kill?"

"He must have, because he killed her the next day."

"What if the same person killed both of them?"

Penny was about to answer in the negative, but changed her mind. "It could be possible. Maybe the killer thought the man and woman were accomplices in whatever crime the man had committed and decided to take them both out."

"When you saw the argument, did the woman seem threatening?"

"No, she didn't. Have you seen her picture? She wasn't very tall or big. It would be foolhardy for her to attack the man."

"I meant in the language she used. Did she make specific threats of any kind? Did she mention who she might alert over his wrongdoing?"

"I didn't hear anything like that. I didn't hear anyone's name," Penny said.

"How were Maura Wells and Warren Topper dressed the night you saw them arguing?"

Penny thought back on the night. "Professionally. I guess that's why I thought they were business colleagues. He wore a blue suit. At least it looked blue. The woman had on a dress and a blazer. Not a fancy dress. It was tailored and businesslike."

"Did Ms. Wells seem upset? Was she crying or emotional?" Lin questioned.

"Not at all. She was angry." The woman checked her phone for the time and said, "I need to get going. I'm staying here at this inn for another five days, if you want to ask me anything else." Penny started away. "Nice talking with you."

Lin returned to the garden beds and began pulling out weeds, her mind in a whirl thinking about what Penny Millbury had told her. Warren and Maura *did* know each other. Did they have some financial interest together that Warren mishandled? He was an investment banker. Did he advise Maura about investing? Did he manage her money? Did he do something wrong with her money?

Another thought came into Lin's head and it made her sit back on her butt.

Did Sofia Rizzo, the woman from Boston who was seeing Warren, think Maura Wells was Warren's wife? Did she decide to kill Warren and his "wife"?

How does it all connect to Elise? Or does nothing connect to Elise?

Lin glanced around the grounds of the inn hoping that the ghost would make an appearance, but no cold air swished over her and Elise did not show up.

How am I going to figure this out?

After two hours working at the inn and hotel, Lin and Nicky got into the truck and drove out of the main part of town over the cobblestone road heading to the next client. Instead of turning left, Lin steered the truck in the opposite direction deciding to take a quick detour up Academy Hill. She parked at the corner, told the dog she'd be right back, and walked a few yards to stand in front of the inn that had once been the old factory building.

Ten minutes passed and Lin gave up so she turned around to go back to her truck when someone at the corner caught her eye and a cold breeze blew against her.

Wearing the usual long, light blue dress, Elise stood shimmering and translucent next to Lin's truck, her face sad.

"You aren't wearing your necklace," Lin said to the ghost.

Elise's hand went to her collarbone and a single tear ran down her cheek.

"Are you buried somewhere in the inn?"

The ghost's expression didn't change.

"Can you lead me to the place where you are buried?" Lin asked softly.

Elise's eyes held Lin's, but still her expression didn't change.

"If I find out who killed Maura Wells and Warren Topper, will it lead me to who killed you?"

The atoms of Elise's form glowed red as blood, swirled like a whirlwind, flared and evaporated.

I'll take that as a "yes".

17

Rosalind McKenna welcomed Lin and Viv into her beautiful, palatial home near Miacomet beach. She led them outside to sit on teak chairs covered with large comfortable white cushions under a flower and vine covered pergola. On the table, cold beverages had been set up in coolers filled with ice. The yard was like something out of a gardening magazine and Lin wanted to ask who did their landscaping.

Rosalind was tall and thin with auburn hair cut to chin-length. "I know Libby from town events. She asked me to have a chat with you. She mentioned you do some research for the town police."

Lin nodded even though what Libby told the woman was not quite accurate. It was a loose arrangement where Lin and Viv reported to Libby what they found out about a case and then Libby would pass it on to her detective friend.

Lin said, "Your friend, Maggie Topper, told us she came to visit you on the day her husband passed away."

"She did, yes. What a stunning turn of events. Warren gone. It's just unbelievable." Rosalind shook her head.

"You've known the Toppers for some time?"

"We met here on-island. It must be nearly twenty years now." Rosalind looked down at her hands. "It is shocking how time flies."

"What were your plans with Maggie that day?" Viv asked.

Rosalind looked up and blinked. "We planned lunch here in the garden, and maybe a drive out to 'Sconset."

"Did you go out to 'Sconset?"

"We didn't. Maggie was later than we'd planned to meet so we just had lunch and sat on the porch talking."

Something about what Rosalind had said picked at Lin. "How did Maggie seem that day?"

"Her usual self," Rosalind said. "I'll modify that. Maggie has seemed tense since around the beginning of August. She has a demanding job. She loves it, but at times, it causes her to stress. When she came for lunch, she was showing signs of stress."

"How so?" Viv asked. "How did her feelings manifest?"

"A little jittery, a little short-tempered, irritable. Distracted. Small things that only a friend would notice."

"And Maggie attributed it to work demands?" Lin asked.

"Maggie never addressed her moods. I noticed her tension and chalked it up to her work."

"You said she was late arriving for lunch?" Viv asked.

"She was. By about forty-five minutes. She told me she was running late."

"Did she say why she was running late?" Lin felt uneasy, but couldn't pinpoint the reason.

"I didn't ask. I assumed she was getting some work done. Maggie works from her house here in Nantucket in the summers. Sometimes, she flies back home for some meetings. It's quite common for working people to do that from here. We're lucky to have such a wonderful airport."

"Has she traveled back and forth a lot this summer?"

"I'd say the usual amount," Rosalind said

"Did you notice anything that seemed to be bothering Maggie lately, maybe other than her work?" Viv asked.

Rosalind adjusted in her seat. "No, I don't think so."

"And how were things between Maggie and Warren?" Lin asked.

The silence stretched out for several long moments.

"How do you mean?" Rosalind asked.

Lin was pretty sure the woman knew what she meant. "Was the marriage strong?"

"I think so," Rosalind said in a soft voice.

"Were there any indications that there might be cracks in the relationship?"

"Did you ask Maggie about this?" Rosalind asked.

"We did talk to her about it," Lin used an easy tone. "We'd like to get your impressions as well. Things don't always go smoothly in life. There are ups and downs. Where were things with Maggie and Warren?"

"I've seen them closer over the years."

"Do you think they were growing apart?" Lin asked.

"They've been married for more than twenty-five

years," Rosalind said and shook her head. "Things can get stale. Marriage has to be worked at."

"Do you think Maggie and Warren were working at their marriage?" Viv questioned.

"I think so." Maggie's voice was weak.

"Were they unfaithful?"

"Oh. I don't know about that. I don't think Warren...."

"Would cheat?" Lin asked.

"I don't think he would."

"Why do you say that?" Viv used an encouraging tone.

Rosalind took in a long breath. "Maggie wouldn't put up with infidelity. Warren had a very nice life. Maggie is very, very wealthy. I don't think Warren would jeopardize his position."

"So Warren wouldn't cheat because he didn't want to lose the money he married into?"

"I know it sounds crass. Warren did very well in his career, very well."

"But?" Lin asked.

"But the level of wealth is different. Maggie is in a different echelon. If Maggie left Warren, his life would never be the same."

"Did Maggie let Warren know that?"

Rosalind rubbed her arm. "I believe she probably did. I enjoy Maggie's company. She's intelligent, well-read, knows everything. And she does not lack confidence, she's hard as nails. It's part of the reason she does so well in business."

"Did Warren have any enemies? Did he have trouble with a client or a colleague?"

"I don't know anything about that." Rosalind gripped the arms of her chair. "He must have had an enemy, right? Someone killed him."

SITTING on Viv's deck under the dark night sky, the cousins ate peanut butter and jam sandwiches with cups of tea while Nicky and Queenie watched fireflies and listened to an owl hoot from the trees a few streets away.

"What did you think of our visit to Rosalind?" Lin blew on her hot tea.

"She was careful. Was it because of her friendship with Maggie or was it because she's afraid of Maggie?"

"Some of both," Lin said. "Maggie seems to be a force to be reckoned with. I would *not* want her in my social circle."

"I don't think you'll ever need to worry about

that." Viv smiled and then took some baby carrots from the plate of cut-up vegetables.

"I don't suppose I do." Lin looked out over the dark yard and at the little white lights Viv had strung along the fence at the back of the property. "What's going on with this case? Maura Wells and Warren Topper knew each other. They argued. Someone killed them ... so they had a common enemy. Why did they? How did they know each other?"

"Investments?" Viv asked. "Did Warren mess up Maura's investments? Did she lose everything she had?"

"Who would kill them? Why?" Lin set her sandwich down. "We've talked about this earlier. Sofia Rizzo, the woman Warren was seeing in Boston, could have killed Warren and Maura. She could have mistaken Maura for Warren's wife."

Viv said, "You told Libby this. She must have shared it with the police. Did they go to talk to this Boston woman? Where was she on the days Maura and Warren were poisoned? Should we go talk to her?"

"If she is the killer, is it smart for us to approach her?" Lin asked. "It might not be a good idea. And how does this killer connect to Elise?"

"Are you sure there is a connection?" Viv asked.

"There is. Definitely. I know it."

Viv added a little sugar to her tea. "How can there be a connection from two hundred years ago to today? I'm baffled."

"Maybe we should focus on researching the past," Lin suggested. "I'm not doing enough to help Elise."

"Okay. So what we know so far is that Elise was Maura Wells's ancestor. Someone killed both of them. Elise's body was never found. Maura was poisoned."

Lin said, "We also know that three men owned the silk factory. Elise worked in the factory. A man named Vernon Willard was the accountant and financial officer of the factory. He made a fortune through investments in businesses. Maggie Topper is related to Vernon Willard."

Viv sat up. "There really are a number of connections between the past and present, but which one will help us find what we're looking for?"

Nicky stood up and let out a growl as Queenie arched her back and hissed.

The doorbell rang and Viv and Lin both jumped.

"Who could that be this late?" Worry washed over Viv's face.

"Should we just sit quietly and hope whoever it is will go away?" Lin was only half-joking.

"Come on." Viv headed into the kitchen to go to the front door. The cat and dog shot past her for the living room.

Viv opened the door with Lin standing right behind her and the two animals pushing around her legs to see who was calling on them.

Maggie Topper stood on the front steps, her eyes blazing and her face looking tense and angry. Her Mercedes was parked at the curb. "Who do you think you are? Rosalind McKenna called and told me what you were asking her about. Really? You have a nerve."

"Would you like to come in?" Viv asked. "Would you like some tea? We can talk."

"No, I would not." Maggie's voice was loud and forceful and she made Viv nervous. "What are you trying to do? Make a mockery of my marriage to Warren? The man is dead. My husband was murdered. Poisoned. And you go around asking if we were unhappy with each other?" Maggie poked the air with her finger. "If you want to do something, then find the murderer. Give my husband some peace. Let me have closure." Tears of frustration welled in the woman's eyes and she batted them away. About to say more, Maggie stopped. She turned and headed down the steps to go to her car. "Just leave me alone. And my friends, too."

Viv quietly shut the door. "Wow," she said softly. "I wasn't expecting that."

Lin was shaken by the woman's brief visit. Her heart raced and a mix of different emotions washed over her. Guilt. Surprise. Some fear at Maggie's tirade. "She knows we're trying to find the killer. The search requires that we talk to people."

"She feels her privacy has been compromised," Viv said, "and so she lashes out."

Unease slipped over Lin's skin and anxiety pulled at her stomach. "I don't like it," she told her cousin. "Lock the door."

18

It was early evening when Jeff met Lin at the bookstore café. As he walked to the table, he smiled at Nicky and Queenie sleeping in their upholstered chair by the bookshelves.

"Those two look comfortable." Jeff took a seat next to Lin, leaned over, and kissed her.

"They've had a hard day," Lin joked. "Queenie spent the day here with Viv, and Nick was busy snoozing in the grass in my clients' yards while I worked."

"Tough lives." Jeff went to the counter to order and returned with a bowl of soup and a coffee. "How is the case coming along?"

"It's stuck." Lin frowned and pushed her books, notes, and laptop to the side. "I don't know what to do next. I've been reading old news articles and history books. I don't know how to find Elise's killer. There's no one alive to interview about it."

"What about Maura Wells and Warren Topper? Is there anything else you can do on that?"

Lin told Jeff about the late-night visitor to Viv's house. "She was steaming angry. It bothered me for the rest of the night. When I went home, I made sure every door and window was locked. I tried to do some crossword puzzles, but I couldn't concentrate. Maggie Topper's face kept popping into my head. I know I was overreacting, but her visit really threw me. We're trying to help. We're not gossips or busy-bodies."

Jeff kidded, "Well, not in this case anyway."

Lin smiled and bopped him lightly with her elbow. "I've been thinking about the note found with Maura Wells on the day she was poisoned. *One down, two to go.* There was no note found with Warren. Why not?"

"There could have been a note, but maybe the killer was in a hurry or people were around, so he couldn't leave it without risking being seen doing it," Jeff said.

"That's a good possibility." Lin fiddled with her pen. "Why hasn't there been an attempt on a third person? The note implies there will be three murders. It's been days since Warren died. Why are things so quiet?"

Jeff rested his soup spoon on a saucer. "It might be because there's too much attention on the crimes right now. When things die down, maybe the third attempt will take place."

Lin nodded. "I was thinking the third victim could be out of reach right now. The person might be off-island or in a situation like being with lots of visiting family or friends that makes it hard for the killer to access him or her. He's biding his time until he can find the victim alone." Making eye contact with Jeff, she said, "Viv and I have been thinking of going to Boston for the day to look up Sofia Rizzo."

"The woman who was having the affair with Topper? The woman you and Viv suspect may have killed Topper and Maura Wells? Are you planning to talk to her or just gather some information on her?"

"We thought it might be helpful to speak with her, but...."

"Lin," Jeff's tone was one of concern. "If she's a killer and you approach her about what's happened here, I don't think she'd hesitate to hurt you."

"I agree. We thought we might just go to Boston and scout around, or Viv wondered about making an appointment with the woman to ask questions about real estate investing. Sofia Rizzo is a real estate attorney."

"Just don't confront her," Jeff cautioned.

Lin pulled over her laptop and kit some keys. "Here are some pictures of her."

There were several photos on the screen of a tall, slim, attractive woman in her late thirties or early forties with long black hair and dark eyes.

"Why would someone put up with a guy who isn't around often and doesn't make a commitment?" Jeff asked.

"That could be all she wanted at first. If she's the killer, what she wanted must have changed over time."

"Or maybe she found out he was married and didn't care to be lied to by cheating Warren," Jeff said.

A little wisp of an idea flickered through Lin's mind, but it was brief and floated away before she could grasp at it.

"Can I see the history book with Elise's picture in it?" Jeff requested.

Lin took the book from her pile and opened it to the page Jeff wanted.

"How old was she when she died?"

"Twenty-six," Lin said.

"And she had a four-year-old daughter?"

"Yes, her name was Elizabeth. She went to live with her aunt on the mainland."

Jeff stared at the picture of Elise in the line of women who worked at the factory. He leaned in closer to get a better look. "Elise is wearing her necklace in the photograph."

"It must have had sentimental value because she wears it frequently," Lin said.

Lifting his eyes to his girlfriend, Jeff said, "You got the impression from Elise that she was killed in the factory, right?"

"Yes. From her reaction when I asked her about it, I would say it was definitely the place where she was murdered."

"Could anyone go into the silk factory or do you think the doors were locked?"

"My guess would be that it would be too distracting for the workers to have people coming and going. Maybe people could enter into the office section of the place, but I'd think the factory part would be off-limits to visitors. Why do you ask?"

"If only workers could be in the factory, then wouldn't it have been a worker who killed Elise?"

Lin's eyes widened. "For some reason, I doubt one of the women killed her and only women worked in factory production, but what about one of the men who handled the business side of things?" She reached for her notebook for the lists of workers from the time. "There were the three owners and the financial officer/accountant. There was a factory manager named Leland Cane and an assistant to him named Daniel Butler. There were men who tended the mulberry bushes and silk worms, but that was located in the Polpis area. What do you think was the motivation?"

Jeff said, "One of the men could have been attracted to Elise, but she didn't reciprocate his feelings."

Lin scowled knowing very well that Jeff's suggestion was a viable, but unfortunate reason.

"What if Elise saw something going on that shouldn't have been and she was killed to keep her quiet."

"Like what?" Lin asked.

Jeff shrugged. "Something illegal? Tampering with the silk products by adding a cheaper thread to the weaving? Cheating the owners in some way? Skimming money from the profits?"

A flush of nervousness raced through Lin's body. "Those are good ideas. I think you're on to something. But how will we ever find out? If the person wasn't caught for wrongdoing and reported on, then the information is lost."

Jeff said, "And killing Elise would have accomplished the killer's objective. Get rid of the witness and the wrongdoing continues."

"It's horrible to even consider. Some monster takes a life to advance his cheating or stealing or whatever his aim was."

"It's not an uncommon event." Jeff's face showed disgust.

Anton bustled around the bookshelves carrying a briefcase, scanned the café section, spotted Lin and Jeff, and hurried over to join them.

"Why don't you answer your phone?" Anton asked. "I texted twice. Finally, I got in touch with Viv and she said you were here." The historian picked up a paper napkin and dabbed at his forehead. "It's still so warm outside."

Lin checked her phone to discover the ringer was off.

"You look like a man in a hurry," Jeff said with a smile.

"I am." Anton unsnapped his briefcase, removed a bunch of papers, and placed them on the table. "I was working in the library all day and suddenly I remembered something. I am in contact with many,

many other historians all over the world and we share information. I have a scholar-friend who lives in Connecticut. In his research, he discovered a trove of old letters to a man who lived in the state in the mid 1800s. Charles Frank was his name. My friend scanned some of the letters for me because they were correspondence between Charles Frank and a man in Nantucket." Anton glanced over at the café counter. "I must get a cup of tea."

Jeff stood. "I'll get it for you."

Lin looked at Anton. "What about the letters?"

"I completely forgot I had the scans of those letters, but for some reason, the thought came to me today while I was researching something else."

Lin asked again. "What about the letters?"

"There are some letters from a man from Nantucket. The year was 1842." Anton paused to look through his briefcase.

"Anton, would you please tell me what this about?"

"The man was Vernon Willard."

Lin's heart pounded double-time.

"In the letters, he discusses his business interests. He mentions the silk factory and the very fortunate position he has obtained there. *Very fortunate* were his words. He talks about the silk production in glowing terms, how profitable the business is. A few months later in a subsequent letter, Mr. Willard mentions that things are taking a turn for the worse at the factory, profits are falling, however, his own situation is improving. Again, I'm quoting his words."

"What does it mean?" Lin asked.

Jeff returned with the tea and set it in front of Anton.

Anton leaned forward with a conspiratorial look on his face. "I believe Mr. Vernon Willard was stealing from the factory."

The historian's next comments were lost on Lin as her ears buzzed. She felt light-headed and gripped the edge of her seat.

"It would take many hours of research to confirm my suspicions," Anton explained, "and I might never be able to find documentation to back up my theory. However, I've been doing this for a long time and have seen similar language in letters and documentation coded to hide the facts of theft, but to allude to self-serving illegal activity."

Jeff said, "The factory failed a few years later. It probably wasn't helped by Vernon Willard stealing profits."

"The mulberry trees did not do well on-island,"

Anton said. "The factory was destined to fail eventually since the silk worms required the mulberry trees. I suspect Mr. Willard hastened the inevitable by diverting some of the profits to his own bank account."

Lin's vision dimmed. *And Elise found out what Vernon Willard was doing and he murdered her to keep her silent.*

19

Wearing her sleep shirt and shorts and with her hair up in a ponytail, Lin sat at her desk in the cottage's guest room that she used for an office when she had some programming work to do for a company on the mainland. It was past midnight and Nicky was sound asleep in the corner.

She'd been thinking about Vernon Willard since she'd left Viv's bookstore earlier in the evening. The man may have been stealing from the factory, squirreling away money and padding his own bank account with it. From Anton's research, they'd discovered information that Willard was unscrupulous in business ... in other words, probably a cheat and a thief.

If Elise found out Willard was stealing and was

about to report it or confront the financial officer about his deeds, he may have done something to silence her, forever.

Walking home from Viv's store, an idea formed that made Lin's heart race. What if Vernon Willard killed Elise and buried her on his acres of property on upper Main Street?

Lin had been hunched over her laptop for an hour going through old land records of Nantucket, Massachusetts and had finally found an entry for a building permit for Willard's house on Main Street. She blinked and stared at the screen.

Vernon Willard received the permit to build on June 18, 1844.

Elise went missing in September, 1843, a year before Willard built his house.

Lin's shoulders slumped in disappointment. Elise couldn't be buried on Willard's property ... he didn't own the place until a year later.

Picking up her phone, she texted Anton asking if there was any way he could find out where Mr. Willard lived while working at the factory before moving into his new house.

With a sigh, she searched the records for the purchase of homes on the island by the silk factory manager, Leland Cane, and by his assistant, Daniel

Butler. In fifteen minutes, Lin found what she was looking for, the addresses for where the men lived when they were employed at the factory.

As she crawled into her bed, Nicky circled three times and then curled up on his cushion in the corner of the room.

At four in the morning, Lin woke from a loud noise and a chill in the room. Sitting up, she saw Nicky standing next to his doggy bed sniffing the air.

Even though her nerves were on high alert, she managed to stay perfectly still, listening.

The house was quiet. "It must have been some kids making noise as they walked past the house or a car with a rough-running engine," Lin told the dog. When she got out of bed to turn off the air conditioning unit, she hesitated and slowly turned around in the dark room expecting to see that Elise was the cause of the cold air, but no spirit was present.

Taking a peek out of each of the bedroom windows, Lin saw the neighbor's house, dark and quiet, and the empty road, and satisfied that nothing was out of the ordinary, she got back into bed and pulled up the blanket.

～

AFTER WORK, Lin showered and changed and then headed out with Nicky walking along the road ahead of her. They followed the lane to Mill Street and, passing well-tended cottages and larger homes with wide lawns and gardens, the young woman and her dog took two more turns before reaching Tangerine Street.

Walking past four or five homes, Lin found the number she was looking for ... a three-story, gray shingled home with window boxes overflowing with pink and blue flowers and a row of blooming hydrangeas in front. In the 1840s, this had been the home of the silk factory's manager, Leland Cane.

To the right of the house, a brick walkway ran under a white arbor leading to the rear of the property. Lin got a peek of the lush lawn, stone patio, green hedges, and flower beds.

Did this man kill you, Elise? Was it Leland Cane who took your life? Did he bury you at the back of his property?

Lin crossed to the other side of the road and waited, pretending to read messages on her phone, but really hoping that Elise would appear.

"Where is she, Nick?" Lin asked. The dog sat next to her leg watching a bird in the tree.

Time passed and the ghost did not make an

appearance. Nicky looked up at his owner and whined.

"Okay. Maybe this house has nothing to do with where Elise is buried. Let's go to the next one."

Lin and the dog made their way to West Dover Street, found the house where the assistant factory manager, Daniel Butler, had lived in the 1840s, and repeated what they'd done at the last home.

She looked down at Nicky who sat lazily at the side of the road glancing around at any movement or sound, someone walking, a squirrel scurrying up the trunk of a tree, a child's laughter.

"Where is Elise, Nick? Will she show up? Was she buried here or is this the wrong place, too?"

After waiting a little longer, Lin decided to move on not wanting to attract the attention of someone who would wonder why she was hanging around the neighborhood.

If Lin found the place Elise was buried, would the ghost show up there? Was she expecting more from Elise than what the spirit was capable of doing? Lin let out a heavy sigh. How would she figure this out? Elise could be buried anywhere on the almost forty-eight square miles of island land.

Deciding to head into town to see Viv at the bookstore, Lin heard her phone buzz and saw a text from Anton. He'd looked through some online historical information created from an old ledger he'd used previously to find where and when certain people had lived on the island.

His text gave Lin an address on Fair Street. Anton discovered that Vernon Willard had rented a home there while working at the silk factory. Part of the dates are obscured on the document he informed Lin, but Willard rented the house for at least part of the time leading up to building his place on upper Main Street.

With new hope and a spring in her step, Lin hurried to the address Anton had sent her. The gray shingled building consisted of three stories, had white shutters next to each window and a shiny black door at the front of the house. Behind the building, Lin spied a bit of grass and a brick patio.

Is this where your bones are buried, Elise? Lin thought. *Is your body here? Did Vernon Willard kill you and bury you behind this house he was renting?*

Lin waited to feel the cold air surround her, but nothing happened. No icy breeze. No spirit.

With a heavy heart and a feeling that she'd failed her ghost, Lin decided to go home.

She fed the dog and then made spaghetti and a pasta sauce, took it outside to the deck, and ate at the teak table alone with her thoughts. In two days, she and Viv planned to take the ferry to the mainland and hop on a bus to Boston where they hoped to see Sofia Rizzo. They'd both agreed not to confront the woman about her relationship with Warren Topper, but only visit the law firm where she worked to try and talk to her about real estate investing. Knowing the woman might not have time to speak with them, they wanted to give it a try anyway.

The sky darkened and the lights for the deck came on and illuminated the space. A chill came over her and made her shiver, and for a few seconds, Lin attributed the coolness to the night air ... and then knew better. She looked around the deck and the patio and then saw the reason for the cold.

Nicky whined and thumped his tail against the deck floor.

Beyond the stone wall, Sebastian Coffin stood in the field on the far side of the patio. Lin jumped up and walked to the edge of the deck.

Her ancestor from long ago, stood still, his eyes connecting with hers and the sensation of cold disappeared.

Lin heard the doorbell ring and the dog let out a loud bark.

Sebastian stared at her, and then deliberately

shook his head back and forth before slowly fading away.

Turning to go inside the house to answer the door, Lin stopped short. *Something's wrong.*

Hurrying into the living room with the dog at her heels, she sidled up to the window and looked out to see who was at her front door.

The porch light lit up the steps. No one was there.

"What's going on?" she whispered to the dog.

Lin unlocked the door, put her hand on the knob, turned it, and opened the door.

Nicky growled and then barked.

Looking down at the stoop, Lin saw the package. She slammed the door, rushed to the kitchen for her phone, and placed an emergency call to the police.

SHORTLY AFTER THE police showed up, Jeff and Viv arrived wearing expressions of alarm.

"What happened?" Jeff hugged his girlfriend.

Lin told them about the package on the stoop. "The officers said there was a container of rat poison inside and whoever left it wasn't trying to poison me, but either wanted to send a warning or was playing a prank."

"A prank?" Viv said with a loud voice. "I don't think so. I think it's a warning to back off the case."

"I agree." Jeff nodded.

"I would be inclined to think it was a prank," Lin said. "Except that I had a visitor a few moments before the bell rang."

"Elise?" Viv asked.

"Sebastian. He looked me in the eye and when the doorbell rang, he shook his head. I knew it was a message to be cautious. That's why I called the police when I saw the box, otherwise I would have picked it up and brought it inside. I was afraid it might be a bomb."

Viv said, "Sebastian might also have been warning you against the person who delivered the poison to your door. Too bad you don't have a surveillance camera on the front of the house."

Lin made tea and the three sat together discussing the situation until the late hour sent Viv and Jeff home. Before leaving, they both invited Lin to come and stay with them, but she declined saying she didn't believe she was in danger.

Hugging Viv goodbye, Lin told her cousin, "Keep your eyes open. We both need to be careful."

20

The Middle Moors of Nantucket island comprised over three thousand acres of open, undeveloped protected space and was made up of three main sections, Altar Rock, the Serengeti, and Pout Ponds. On the western end of the moors, the Pout Ponds area consisted of kettle ponds that Native Americans believed were footprints of a giant that had filled with water to make the ponds.

To the south, the four hundred acres of the Serengeti resembled a large plain of low-growing brush and vegetation along with a few trees. From the Milestone Road, the wooden cutouts of gazelle, lions, and zebras that people had placed in the fields could be seen grazing in the grasses.

One of the highest elevations on the island, Altar

Rock provided gorgeous views of the harbor, the village of 'Sconset, two lighthouses, and the moorlands.

With miles and miles of dirt roads, paths, and bike trails, the moors was a popular place for dog walkers, hikers, and bikers, and Lin and Jeff loved to bike and walk in the area for the beauty and peacefulness of the space.

The sun was lower in the sky and the early evening temperature was pleasantly cooler than the day had been. The young couple rode their bikes to the moors and after locking them, headed along the sandy paths to Altar Rock to admire the views.

"I love it here," Lin told her boyfriend. "I'm glad you were finished with work for the day so we could hike a little. I need to clear my head."

"I've always loved the moors," Jeff said. "There's something almost spiritual about this area. I can feel any tension or stress just drop away when I'm out here."

"I've been thinking a lot about Elise," Lin said. "Even if we find her bones, we'll never know how she was killed or who did it. From what Anton told us, I bet the killer is Vernon Willard. Historical accounts mention the man's unscrupulous nature and the underhanded ways he built his fortune.

He'll never be punished for his evil deeds. Elise can't cross over. Her spirit has stayed in the inn building for almost two hundred years. It makes me so sad."

Jeff took her hand. "Elise has finally found someone who can see her. I know the innkeepers catch glimpses of her, but it's not the same way you see her. It must be a comfort and a relief. I don't think it matters to Elise that her killer won't be brought to justice. I think what matters is for one person to know that her life was taken, for one person to know what happened to her even if the details can't be realized, for one person who will search for her bones." Jeff squeezed Lin's hand. "That person is you."

Lin stopped walking and turned to her boyfriend.

"You and your ability to help ghosts ... you're a blessing, Lin Coffin."

Wrapping Jeff in her arms, Lin rested her head on his shoulder. "Thank you for that," she whispered. "I needed it more than you know."

∾

WHEN THEY RETURNED from their hike, Lin and Jeff walked down to the docks to visit with Viv and John on his boat. The lights twinkled off the water and a soft breeze gently moved the warm air around them.

John lit some candles and brought out drinks and munchies and the four of them sat around chatting and watching the people walk along the docks past the boats.

"I got a new listing today," John told his companions with excitement in his voice. "And it's going to be a monster commission for me when it sells."

"Where is it," Jeff asked. "Which house?"

"It's on upper Main Street. A fabulous house with five acres of land."

Lin sat up. "Who owns it?"

"You know that guy who was poisoned? His wife, Maggie Topper. She wants to sell the place. She told me she's had enough of the island. She can't stay here with the awful memory of her husband's murder."

"You're kidding me," Viv said. "She's selling?"

"Do you know her?" John looked surprised.

Lin said, "Maggie seemed like she was devoted to that house. Her ancestor had the place built nearly two hundred years ago. She seemed so connected to the property. I can't believe it."

"Well, whatever you do, don't change her mind,"

John told them. "She wants me to list the place right after her husband's memorial service."

Lin and Viv sat in stunned silence while John talked to Jeff about some changes he wanted to make to the galley below deck.

"Do you have time to take on a job like that?" John asked.

"Let's go see it," Jeff suggested.

The men went below to discuss the project.

Viv got up and moved to the chair next to her cousin. "Maggie's selling?" she asked. "I'm shocked."

"I suppose it's understandable. Her husband was murdered here. She must be crushed by what happened and just can't be here anymore," Lin said.

"Still, it's very unexpected. I didn't think that woman would ever sell the house," Viv said.

"The Toppers didn't have children so maybe Maggie has no one to leave the place to. She must have decided there was no reason to keep it," Lin said. "We've been focusing on Topper's infidelity as the reason for his and Maura's murders. We haven't paid attention to other reasons for the poisonings."

"Do you have other ideas?"

"What about the Topper's friend, Paul Monroe?" Lin asked.

Viv's eyebrows went up. "Paul Monroe? Why?"

"He made a point to come sit with us at the music event. He seemed like he'd had too much to drink. Was it a put-on? Did he confide in us that Warren had a woman in Boston to make us think the woman killed Warren after finding out he was married?"

"You think Paul had something to do with the poisonings?"

"It's not too farfetched, is it?"

"What would be his motivation to kill?" Viv asked.

"Paul could have been having an affair with Maggie. Remember I felt like there was some awkward tension between them when he showed up while we at her home? Were they awkward because Paul thought Maggie would be alone and when he saw us, he had to come up with a reason to have arrived unexpectedly?"

"Wow. It did seem like Maggie wasn't that attached to Warren and Maggie's friend implied the same thing. Maybe Maggie was bored with Warren and needed some excitement. But why would Paul kill Warren?" Viv asked. "Maggie could have just divorced her husband and taken up with Paul."

"Maybe Maggie didn't see Paul as a long term thing. She may have only wanted a fling. Paul might have thought if he got rid of Warren, Maggie might have turned to him for a permanent relationship."

"That could be. I completely overlooked Paul. He should be a suspect. Wait. If Paul killed Warren, who killed Maura?"

"Paul might have killed Maura to throw suspicion off of him. It makes the murders more complicated. It keeps eyes off of him." Lin said, "If Maggie suspects Paul was behind Warren's death, maybe she's worried about her affair becoming public. That could be why she was so angry with us. We're getting too personal. She might be afraid we'll expose her affair. But there's a problem with Paul as a suspect. How does he connect to Elise and who would be his third victim?"

Viv stared out over the water and after a minute, she said, "I have no idea. Is there anyone else we should be considering?"

Lin took a deep breath. "What about Rosalind McKenna."

"Really?"

"Lots of people lie. Rosalind seemed reluctant to tell us Maggie wasn't actually thrilled about life with Warren, but maybe she was pretending. Maybe she made up that story to throw suspicion off of herself."

"Why would Rosalind kill Warren?" Viv asked.

"An affair with him gone wrong?"

"And she killed Maura, too?"

"I don't know." Lin said. "There's another thing that's bothering me. We're looking at this from only one side. What if the killer was after Maura specifically and Warren was secondary? Someone may have targeted Maura and linked her to Warren so they both had to die."

Viv rubbed her temple. "This whole thing is a like a giant ball of thread and every time we pull at a piece, it gets tangled up with four more pieces."

"There's another question I have."

"My head hurts." Viv rolled her eyes. "Why do I think what you're about to say is going to make everything worse?"

"We can come up with theories for why Warren and Maura were killed. But the note found on Maura said *one down, two to go*. How do any of our theories include a third victim?"

Viv pressed her lips together for several seconds and sighed. "They don't."

21

The morning sun was strong as the passengers waiting for the ferry stood in a line on Straight Wharf while the people on the boat from Hyannis disembarked.

Lin and Viv wore casual dresses and carried light sweaters for their trip to Boston.

Viv was telling her cousin about how busy the bookstore-café had been recently and how she hoped to have her best September yet when Lin noticed someone walking towards them pulling a small, wheeled suitcase.

Giving Viv a jab with her elbow, Lin said, "Look. Is that who I think it is?"

Viv moved her gaze to a young woman in her late thirties with shoulder-length dark hair, tanned skin, and dark eyes. Wearing a red dress and black heels, the attractive woman had just stepped off the ferry from the mainland.

"Well, gosh," Viv said. "It's Sofia Rizzo. She just saved us from a long day trip to see her." Narrowing her eyes, she asked, "Why the heck is she here?"

"Let's go find out." Lin ducked under the rope that contained the waiting ferry riders and started after the woman.

Hurrying after her cousin, Viv asked, "What are we going to say to her?"

Lin smoothed her hair and put on her sunglasses as she moved alongside Sofia. "Oh, excuse me, aren't you Sofia Rizzo?"

The dark-haired woman slowed and looked at Lin. "Yes, I am. Do we know each other?"

"We've not been introduced. My cousin and I were acquaintances of Warren Topper," Lin fibbed. "Warren was a friend of yours, wasn't he?"

Sofia's face hardened. "Was. Past tense."

"I'm sorry for the loss of your friend," Viv said.

"He was no longer my friend," Sofia muttered.

"Are you here for vacation?" Lin asked not wanting the woman to walk away.

"Not really. I'm here to talk to the police."

Lin wasn't expecting that response. "Is every-thing okay?"

Viv said, "Lin and I do case research for the police on a part-time basis. We've done some work on Mr. Topper's and Maura Wells's cases."

Sofia looked at them. "Have you learned anything important?"

Lin stopped walking and extended her hand. "I'm Carolin Coffin. This is my cousin, Vivian Coffin. Do you have time to get a coffee with us?"

Sofia assessed them and their invitation and said, "Okay. My meeting at the police station isn't for an hour and I can't check in at my hotel yet."

The three women sat in a café on Easy Street and after ordering coffees, Lin asked, "Have you been to the island before?"

"I haven't. This is my first visit."

"Did the police ask you to come?"

"No. I called them and asked to meet with them."

"Why?" Viv asked.

Sofia shifted in her chair. "I probably shouldn't say."

Lin told the young woman that they were among the first to arrive at Maura Wells's murder scene and that they'd interviewed several people in regards to the deaths.

"What have you been able to uncover?" Sofia asked.

"Some interesting facts and details," Lin said pointedly, making eye contact with Sofia.

The waiter came with the drinks and set them down.

"You knew Warren for a couple of years?" Lin asked.

Sofia blew out a breath knowing full well that Lin and Viv probably knew about her relationship with Warren. "Yes. A little over two years."

"You were close friends?" Viv asked.

Sofia gripped her mug with both hands. "You could say that."

"Until recently?" Lin asked. "You broke off the friendship?"

"I did." Taking a long swallow of the coffee, Sofia set the mug down with a loud thunk. "Have you ever been deceived?" She didn't wait for answers. "It isn't pretty. It's upsetting and unsettling. To trust someone, to think you know them, and then discover you've been deceived ... well, you begin to question everything you've ever thought. You start to think there must be something faulty in your decision-making skills, in your ability to judge a person or a situation."

Viv said, "It's not easy to open yourself to another

person, and then to find out they aren't who you thought they were, well, it's a shock."

"You can say that again." Sofia looked down at her coffee.

"You didn't know Warren was married?" Lin asked gently.

Sofia's head popped up. "Absolutely not. That liar. I must look pretty stupid not to have figured it out."

"Not at all. Warren Topper seems to have been a very skillful liar," Lin said. "It seems he was able to hide his deception for years. How did you find out?"

"I started to become suspicious of him. He never wanted to be in the public eye with me, like at a company function or a charity event. If he went to anything like that, he wouldn't arrive or depart with me. He said he didn't like public displays of affection so he never acted like we were anything more than colleagues. I started to wonder why he behaved like that. It was a bunch of little things that finally added up. I can't believe I never did an internet search on the man until the end ... and when I did, I nearly fainted dead away."

"Did you confront him?" Lin asked.

"I sure did. I didn't know I could be so angry. I let

him have it with both barrels. He didn't even apologize. I told him to get out, and he did. He didn't even look back." Sofia's eyes welled up. "I'm not upset about getting rid of him. I'm upset for wasting two years on a monster." Sofia sighed. "When I found out he'd been killed ... I know how awful it is for me to say this ... but, I was glad someone murdered him. I was glad he was dead. The disgusting monster was gone. He couldn't hurt or manipulate anyone else ever again."

"Did you know Maura Wells?" Viv questioned.

"I didn't, but...."

"But?" Lin asked, watching Sofia's face.

"I was away on business when Warren was killed. I was in Spain on business with some colleagues from the real estate firm. I got an email from a woman named Maura Wells."

Lin sat up straight.

Sofia continued, "When I returned from the trip, I found out Ms. Wells had been murdered here on Nantucket the day before Warren was poisoned."

"What did she say in the email?" Lin asked.

"She said she knew I was seeing Warren Topper and she had some important information to share with me about him. I thought it was some scam, like she might be trying to blackmail me. I didn't answer and she didn't reach out to me again. I was honestly horrified when I learned the woman had been killed."

"What do you think Maura Wells wanted to tell you? That Warren was cheating on you?" Viv questioned.

"That was probably what it was about. She most likely wanted to tell me Warren was married."

"Why though? What did it matter to her? Did Warren ever mention Maura Wells to you?" Lin asked.

"No, he didn't. I never heard the name until I received her email," Sofia said.

"We've heard that Warren and Maura might have known each other," Viv said. "We learned that someone overheard Warren and Maura arguing down by Brant Point. The person thought it was a professional argument, that maybe Warren had been handling Maura's investments and something went terribly wrong. Maybe he stole from her or maybe he lost all of her money."

Sofia lifted her mug to her lips. "I never allowed Warren to handle my money. From what I knew, he was knowledgeable and more than capable of managing money. Knowing how devious Warren was, my guess would be that he stole Ms. Wells's investment money and she found out. He would have been in deep trouble." Leaning forward and with a soft voice, Sofia asked, "Is it possible Warren murdered Maura Wells to keep her quiet about his mishandling of her money?"

A shiver of anxiety ran through Lin's body. "That could very well be possible."

Sofia groaned and leaned her head into her hand. "I was not only seeing a lying cheater, but I might have been dating a killer."

"Did Warren ever behave in a way that frightened you?" Lin asked. "Was he ever abusive? Physically or verbally?"

"No, he wasn't. He would be adamant over his restrictions about seeing me, where we could go, when we could go, but he never lost his temper or acted threatening."

"Did he seemed worried about anything? Did he confide in you about his finances?"

"He never talked about money. He never confided in me about anything," Sofia said shaking her head. "You'd think that him never getting close to me or opening up to me would be a red flag. It took me two years to figure it all out."

"It's easy to look back and see things," Lin said. "It's much harder to see those things when you're in the middle of it."

Viv said, "If we're tossing around the possibility that Warren might have killed Maura, then that brings up an important question. If Warren killed Maura to hide his theft of her money, then who killed Warren?"

Lin added, "And *why* did someone kill him?"

22

"Is your truck parked outside?" Viv hurried over to the table where Lin was having tea and a blueberry muffin. She'd gotten up earlier than usual and decided to go to the bookstore for her morning cup of tea before heading to the first landscaping client of the day.

"I got a spot right out front." Lin smiled. "The benefits of waking up before sunrise."

"Can you drive some baked goods over to the inn? Mallory usually does it for me, but she's sick and isn't coming in. I can't do it. We're short-handed without Mallory. I can't leave. It's the busiest time of the day." The innkeeper of the Seaborne Inn had hired Viv temporarily to provide baked goods each morning for the guests' breakfasts. The inn's usual baker was having minor surgery and would be out for two weeks, and Viv was happy to fill in.

Wiping her hands on her napkin, Lin stood up. "Of course, I can. I'll leave Nicky here and come back for him after the delivery."

Lin loaded trays and boxes into the truck and drove the short distance to the inn. It was less than a quarter mile away and was an easy walk, but there were too many items to carry so a vehicle was necessary to transport the goods each morning.

Pulling into the small driveway behind the innkeepers' car, Lin cut the engine and got out. Before removing the things from the truck, she took a moment to let her eyes wander over the outside of the inn. It was hard to believe the beautiful building had started out as a factory where people worked to pay their rent and feed their families.

Shifting her eyes to the lower part of the inn that housed the basement, a shudder ran through Lin as she thought about a young woman losing her life in that space. She'd hoped to see Elise when she dropped off the baked goods, but so far, she hadn't made an appearance.

Holding several big boxes, Lin rang the bell and, with a warm smile, Patricia opened the door to greet her. "Come in, Lin. Viv called to tell me you were bringing the bakery items over." She took two of the boxes from Lin's arms and led the way to the kitchen. "Just in time, too. A few of the guests have started coming down for breakfast."

Lin made two more trips to the truck.

Patricia was busy at the counter removing muffins and slices of banana and cranberry breads from the boxes and placing them on colorful platters. "Come into the dining room and sample some of the things. Milton is trying two new recipes today, one for a quiche and the other for pancakes and he'd like some feedback."

Lin protested, but Patricia gently took her by the arm and escorted her to the dining room. "I know you must have a long day of landscaping work to do. You need your strength, so eat up and let me know what you think about Milton's new selections."

An older couple who sat at the dining room enjoying their breakfasts gave Lin smiles and a pleasant hello. Feeling underdressed in her shorts, tank top, and work boots, Lin took a plate of food to eat in the sitting room. A pretty young woman in her mid-thirties with strawberry blond hair and green eyes sat near the fireplace with a plate of eggs and toast and a cup of coffee.

"Do you mind if I sit?" Lin asked.

"Not at all." The woman gave a nod and although she made a few pleasant comments about how beautiful the island was and how she wished she could stay longer, Lin felt a distinct sense of sadness from her.

"Are you here on a short vacation?"

No, I'm Bridget Wells. I'm the sister of the woman who was poisoned here several days ago."

Lin almost toppled out of her chair. "I'm so very sorry."

"I'm here to collect her body and take her back to Chicago."

Lin murmured more words of condolence. "I didn't know Maura had a sister."

Bridget looked pleased that a stranger remembered her sister's name. "Maura was a researcher, a professor of history. We had ancestors that once lived on Nantucket. I've never been here before."

"I'm sorry your visit isn't under more pleasant circumstances."

"I'd like to come back some day. Maura had an interest in finding out more about our ancestors. She was looking into the life of our great-great-great-grandmother, Elise Porter. She worked in this building when it was a factory."

Lin's heart pounded. "Did your sister find out anything more about her?"

"Elise disappeared in 1843. Her body was never found. Strange, isn't it?" Bridget dabbed at her eyes with her napkin and shook her head in sadness. "An ancestor of ours met with an unfortunate end here on the island and centuries later, my sister was killed here." The woman shook her head. "I have a four-year-old daughter, Ellen. Now that Maura is gone, my daughter and I are the only ones left in the family. I'm almost superstitious about bringing her here. I know it's silly, but if we come to visit, will something happen to her, or me?"

Lin nodded. "It's understandable that you would have that worry. I'd probably feel the same way."

Bridget lifted her cup and sipped. "Maura never married. My sister was always busy studying and teaching and researching. She hoped to marry someday. She would have liked to have children, but she was already forty." Bridget's face hardened. "Unfortunately, Maura got caught up with someone who didn't have her best interests at heart."

A zing of unease raced across Lin's skin. "How do you mean?"

"She was in a relationship with Warren Topper,

the man who was poisoned the day after Maura died."

Lin's hand shook almost spilling her tea. "Maura? And Warren?"

"She'd been with him for almost three years. He was secretive, didn't want to be seen places with Maura. He lived in New York and traveled on business all the time. Maura suggested he move to Chicago or she move to New York so they could see each other more, but Warren wasn't having it. I was suspicious of him. I've read about guys who have families in two different places." She shook her head. "Well, this guy was married and he had Maura in Chicago and another woman in Boston. Warren had been married for over twenty-five years. It's disgusting."

Lin's eyes bugged. "Maura knew this?"

"She found out not long ago. She even emailed the woman in Boston about meeting together to talk. Maura didn't say exactly why in the email. The other woman never answered. My sister wanted to warn her about Warren. Maura came to Nantucket to confront him."

Lin thought about Warren and Maura's argument down at Brant Point. The heated discussion ensued because Maura found out Warren was a liar and a cheat and she was calling him out on it.

"Your sister must have been devastated," Lin said.

"She certainly was. She was heartbroken ... at first. Then she was angry, with Warren *and* with herself for falling for his lies."

"Have you talked with the police?" Lin asked. "Have you informed them about Maura's relationship with Warren?"

"I spoke with them yesterday."

"Did your sister contact Warren's wife to tell her what her husband had been up to?" Lin questioned.

"No. Maura didn't want to get involved with that. She thought the wife must know about his affairs and didn't care. How could that guy carry on with other women for years and his wife not know?" Bridget rubbed at the back of her neck. "I suppose it could be possible that she was unaware. Who cares? I pity that woman living with such a disgusting, selfish human being. Even if she didn't know about his infidelity, she must have realized after years of marriage that the guy was a useless, good-for-nothing low-life. She stayed with him. She must have deserved him."

Lin got up and moved to the chair next to Bridget. "Do you have any idea who might have poisoned your sister? Was she afraid of anyone?"

Bridget said, "She wasn't afraid of Warren, but really? Who knows what someone is capable of doing when he's pushed too far?"

"Do you think Maura's confrontation with him pushed him to the brink? Do you think he could have killed your sister?"

"Maura called me after she met with Warren. She said he was upset, nervous that Maura would reveal his indiscretions to the news outlets. His wife has loads of money, runs a company. Warren had a reputation as a successful investment analyst and financial advisor. The bad press would have done him a lot of damage. Could he have killed Maura? I just don't know."

"Would Maura have gone to the press about Warren?"

"No. She didn't want the invasion of privacy she would have suffered if she fed the story to the news outlets. She'd already suffered enough from being with Warren, from trusting him. What he did was such a terrible betrayal."

Lin realized she had to leave to go pick up Nicky and make it on time to her first client of the day. "I'm sorry for everything that's happened. Maybe I'll see you again."

"It was nice to talk to you," Bridget said. "Thank you for listening."

Lin left the room to pick up the empty delivery boxes and trays from the kitchen to bring back to the bookstore-café. Patricia stood at the counter ladling yogurt into a cut-glass bowl.

"What was the verdict on the quiche and new pancakes?" the innkeeper asked.

"An A-plus to both of them. Delicious. Thank you for the breakfast," Lin said.

"Anytime." Patricia wiped the edge of the bowl.

Before turning for the door, Lin asked, "Have you seen your ghost lately?"

Patricia looked at Lin, her forehead scrunched in thought. "You know, I haven't. It's been quiet around here. Maybe she left us?"

A flash of worry gripped Lin ... she was pretty sure Elise had not left to cross over.

Then where was she?

23

Stakes pounded into the ground indicated where the two white tents would go for Warren Topper's memorial service. New garden beds were in process of being created by Lin and Leonard that would border the sides of the tents, and additional flowers were being added to the already existing beds. Two three-tier outdoor fountains would be installed later in the week and a stone walkway had been put in leading from the back of the house to the tent where the service would be held.

"A lot of money is being spent on this one-day event." Leonard looked around the property with a disapproving look. He'd just pushed a wheelbarrow with two hydrangeas from his truck to a spot in the beds. "Is it a waste to do this or am I old-fashioned?"

"Well, maybe you are old-fashioned, but this seems way over the top." Lin leaned on the end of a shovel. "I guess you could call it a celebration of a life."

"Still." Leonard hauled the bushes out of the wheelbarrow. "When I die, don't let anybody do something like this for me."

Lin smiled. "Don't worry. No one you know has the money to do something like this."

Leonard grunted. "Ah, the benefits of not being wealthy."

Nicky followed the older man back and forth from the truck to the rear of the house as he retrieved more bushes and flowers. "What's Maggie Topper going to do with all these plants once the service is over?"

"Probably toss most of them away. Once the service is over, the fountains and new beds are going to look out of place when the tents come down." Lin shrugged. "The property is going on the market the day after the service."

"It will fetch a pretty penny," Leonard stated. "Did Ms. Topper pay us yet?"

"Half. The second half is due on completion."

"Keep an eye on her, Coffin. Make sure she doesn't skip town without paying us."

Lin chuckled. "I assume she's good for it."

"You never know." Leonard headed back to the truck for the last load and when he returned, he asked, "You okay putting these in so I can go to the next client?"

"I can do it." Lin passed the back of her hand over her forehead to remove perspiration. The day was unseasonably warm with a clear, blue sky and a bright sun beating down on the young woman. "You're going to handle the heavier planting tomorrow. If we split up the work, we won't fall behind with the other clients."

The work on Maggie's yard was going well and the new landscaping designs were on track to be completed over the next two days.

Lin told her partner about meeting Sofia Rizzo in town by the ferry dock and running into Maura Wells's sister, Bridget, at the inn.

"You've had two interesting meetings lately," Leonard said chugging from a water bottle. "But what they told you doesn't help to identify Warren Topper's or Maura Wells's killer. Or should I say killers?"

"Do you think there are two killers?" Lin asked.

Leonard rubbed his chin. "I can see why Warren would be a good suspect in Maura's death. He probably worried she would reveal his cheating and that it would ruin his life. He might have been pretty desperate to keep his liaisons a secret."

"What about Warren though? Maura found out he was a cheater and a liar, but she died before him so she couldn't have been his murderer. Sofia found out about Warren's lies, too. She may have been so upset that she decided to put an end to his antics once and for all." Lin paused and said, "But, she didn't strike me as a killer."

Leonard said, "What about the friend? Paul Monroe? He could have had something to do with Warren's murder. Maybe some business thing between them went bad. Maybe Paul has a thing for Maggie and wanted Warren out of the way."

Lin nodded and let out a sigh. "Where's Elise? I haven't seen her for a couple of days. The innkeeper at the Seaborne Inn told me she hasn't had a glimpse of the ghost for a while. Why doesn't she appear to me?" Lin's voice trembled. "Have I done something wrong? Have I taken too long to figure out where she's buried? Has she given up on me being able to help her?"

Leonard put his arm around his partner's shoulders and gave her a squeeze. "Nonsense, Coffin. Time is probably immaterial to a ghost. You haven't done anything wrong. Elise hasn't given up on you."

Lin batted at her eyes and sniffled. "I don't want to let her down."

"You won't. And I know you. You'll work on this for the rest of your life, if you have to. Once a spirit puts his or her trust in you, they're in your heart until you find what they need." Leonard playfully pat Lin on the head. "Now get back to work. We got things to do."

Lin smiled at the man. "Thanks for the pep talk."

"Okay. I'll head out now. Text me if you need anything."

Lin walked across the lawn to the back porch of the house. She'd left her cooler in the shade of the porch and unzipped the top to retrieve her water container. Pulling out a bowl, she poured some water into it and set it on the grass for the dog and then took three long swallows from the bottle before returning it to the cooler.

"I wish there was a little shade where I'm working," Lin said to the dog as they headed back to the landscaping work.

Another two hours passed and in that time, she'd finished planting six bushes and all of the flowers for that particular bed. Her tank top stuck to her back from the sweat and small smears of soil showed on her arms.

Stepping back to admire the work, a whoosh of freezing air swept around her and she turned to see who had arrived.

Sebastian stood off to the side near a grove of trees, the old ghost keeping his eyes pinned on his descendant.

Lin waited to see if he'd come closer and when he didn't budge, she started towards him. The sound of the porch door closing at the rear of Maggie Topper's house made her stop and look back.

Maggie waved from the porch and hurried over to speak to Lin. The woman wore a crisp white blouse, a tight pale blue skirt, and sandals. Her hair seemed to have been professionally dried and styled.

"I'm leaving the house shortly," Maggie said. "I'm going to the mainland overnight." She glanced around at the landscaping work. "I see things are taking shape. Good. Do you need anything before I go? Do I need to clarify anything about what I want done?"

"I think we're all set. I have the design plans in the briefcase next to my cooler." Lin gestured towards the porch. "I can refer to them if I need to."

Nicky sat at Lin's feet and let out a whine.

Although Lin knew the plans very well, Maggie discussed what she wanted next to the second tent as if the young landscaper had never heard the information previously. While Lin humored the woman by listening to the details for the hundredth time, and even though she still felt the cold chill brought only by a spirit, she took a quick glance over her shoulder to where Sebastian had been standing to see if he was still there.

The ghost was gone.

Disappointed, she started to turn her attention back to Maggie, but stopped. Something glimmered in the spot where Sebastian had been.

Elise. Her form was a glittering, see-through assemblage of atoms.

Lin smiled.

Lifting her arm, Elise placed her hand against her throat. Her necklace was still missing.

"Lin? Did you hear what I said about this spot next to the tent?" Maggie looked impatiently at the young woman.

"What did you say?"

Letting out a slight sigh of exasperation and with a hand on her hip, Maggie repeated her instructions.

"Right. Yes." Lin nodded. "Got it."

"Are you sure I shouldn't say it again?" Maggie's eyes squinted in the sunlight.

"No need," Lin assured her. "I understand."

Lin's heart nearly stopped when she noticed what was at Maggie's neck. A beautifully-cut silver necklace encircled the woman's throat.

Barely able to get the words out, Lin eyed the piece of jewelry and said, "That's lovely."

Maggie's hand went to the necklace. "Thank you. It's an antique. My ancestor, Vernon Willard, the man who had my house built, once owned it. He gave it to my great-great-great-grandmother. It's been passed down through the generations. I'm very fortunate to have it."

The necklace sparkled like it was made of a thousand diamonds and the brightness of it cut into Lin's optic nerve. Her vision dimmed and she took a couple of steps back.

Maggie's eyes narrowed. "Are you okay?"

"Yes. It's just the heat." Lin was familiar with the necklace clasped around Maggie's neck ... and she knew how it got into Vernon Willard's hands. He stole it. He ripped it from Elise's throat, after he strangled her to death.

Lin's face flushed with rage. "Your ancestor? Vernon Willard. He obtained that necklace?"

As a haughty expression spread over her face, Maggie's fingers ran along the edge of the silver chain. "He did. It's quite old. It's from nearly two hundred years ago."

"Do you know how he got it?" Lin demanded.

"Not exactly. I assume he bought it in a store," Maggie said with a smug smile.

"In a store? Is that what you think? Do you assume that?" Lin's blood boiled.

Maggie's expression changed to one of slight wariness. "How else would he have acquired it?"

Lin glared at the woman. "Did you know Maura Wells?"

"What? No, I didn't."

"How about Sofia Rizzo? Are you familiar with that name?"

"No, I'm not." Something flashed over Maggie's face and she looked at Lin like something was wrong with her. "I'm late," she said practically spitting out the words. "I need to get going." The woman turned on her heel and hurried away to the house.

24

Muttering under her breath, Lin kicked at an empty flower container and sent it tumbling over the grass. Glancing around the rear yard, she searched for Elise, but the ghost was gone. She grabbed her tools from the ground and piled them next to one of the beds, then raced to the porch to get her cooler. Her work day was now done. Lin could not bear to be on the property that once belonged to a murderer, a murderer who amassed his money by lying and stealing and cheating.

Sweat trickled down the side of her face, partly from the heat and partly from fury. Vernon Willard killed Elise. He stole her necklace and kept it in his family like some trophy he gloated over. It sickened

Lin. Her stomach roiled and her vision sparkled. Feeling weak, she sank onto the porch's granite top step and pulled her cooler closer noticing she'd forgotten to zip the lid closed.

Reaching inside, she removed her water bottle and poured some of it into the dog's bowl.

Nicky sat on the grass in front of her, watching his owner.

"Here, Nick. Have a drink." Lin gestured to the bowl and the dog stood, his fur ruffled, and he barked again and again.

"I know. He killed Elise."

The ghost-woman suddenly appeared a few yards from the porch creating a wave of cold air that surrounded Lin.

Lin stood. "Maggie has your necklace. It's been passed down in the family from that monster, Vernon Willard." Lin rubbed at her forehead. "I'd like to rip it from her throat."

As Lin lifted her water bottle towards her lips, Elise's atoms flared a blinding red. The atoms swirled like a tornado and the force of the wind knocked Lin off her feet and flung her onto the ground, the bottle flying from her hand and hitting the grass.

Pushing herself up, Lin groaned and shook her head. The ghost was gone.

"What the...?" Lin leaned forward onto her knees, feeling shaky and confused. Reaching for the water bottle with the intention of pouring some into her hand to splash over her face, Nicky darted to her, barking.

Lin froze. The water. The dog hadn't touched what was in his bowl. Elise's whirlwind disappearance had knocked the bottle from her hand. A smothering tidal wave of fear crashed over her and she sat back, stunned and horrified.

Poison.

Lin frantically rubbed her hand in the grass to remove any drops of water.

Maggie.

Jumping to her feet, Lin clenched her fists and stared at the back door of the house.

"She tried to poison us," Lin whispered. "Maggie. She poisoned Maura. She poisoned Warren." Dashing to her cooler, she dumped everything out of it, ripped the wrapping from her sandwich, hurried to where the bottle rested on the grass, and used the wrap to carefully pick it up and put it in the cooler. She then used two napkins from her lunch box to gently lift the dog's bowl and place it in the bottom of the cooler, and then zipped the top closed.

Lin looked for her phone to call the police. Where was it? Lin shuffled through the things from the cooler she'd dumped onto the porch.

No phone.

I left it near the cooler. Bubbles of rage rose in her chest. *Maggie took it.*

With her heart pounding, Lin looked up to the windows of the house, and then whispered to the dog, "Let's get out of here."

The two took off running from the backyard around to the front driveway and when they reached it, they stopped short.

Maggie stood in the driveway beside her late husband's black BMW, her face contorted with hate and fury. The BMW's trunk was open. "Where do you think you're going?"

The fur on Nicky's neck stood up and he let out a menacing growl.

"To the police." With the dog at her heels, Lin started towards the far side of the long driveway to head for the street.

"Stop right there." Maggie held a gun in her hand and it was pointing right at Nicky.

With her teeth clenched, Lin stepped in front of

her little dog and gestured for him to stay behind her. "Really? You're going to shoot my dog? You pathetic witch."

"Get in the trunk." Maggie used the gun to point to the car. "Or you can watch me shoot your dog before I shoot you."

Lin began to inch towards the woman. "Or, I'll jump you and my dog can watch me shoot you."

"Stop. Stand still. You'll do as I say." Maggie's eyes were wild and her hand seemed to shake slightly.

Lin stopped.

"Keep your distance from me. Walk slowly to the trunk. Very slowly." Maggie gestured to the vehicle. The bright sun glinted off of her gun. "Get going. Small steps."

"Stay with me, Nick," Lin said softly and began shuffling to the back of the car. When she was a few feet from the BMW, she made a hand gesture and the dog slipped under the vehicle.

"Get in the trunk," Maggie demanded.

Lin knew the odds of surviving if a person left a scene with an attacker and was taken elsewhere. Those odds weren't good.

"Get in," the woman screeched.

"How? How should I lie down?" Lin played dumb hoping to get Maggie to come closer.

"Just get in." Maggie seethed and when she took one step forward to give Lin a push, Lin wheeled with her arm raised, and used her elbow to ram it into the woman's face. Maggie shrieked and blood trickled from her nose.

Although the woman staggered, she did not drop the gun, but Lin had enough time to rush to the other side of the vehicle for cover.

Sputtering and muttering, Maggie ran her hand over her nose to wipe at the blood. Her eyes blazed with madness. When the woman moved to the side of the BMW where Lin stood, the young landscaper dashed to the front of the vehicle as if it were a game of musical chairs. Maggie moved to the front and Lin moved to passenger side.

Furious with frustration, Maggie moved back to the driver's side of the car, lifted her hand and shot through the windows of the BMW hoping to hit Lin standing on the passenger side. The window glass shattered with a roar, but Lin had ducked down just in time to miss being hit by the bullet.

Maggie let out a curse.

The sound of an engine reached Lin's ears and in

three seconds, Leonard's truck came into view as it came down the long driveway.

Lin frantically waved and pointed at Maggie so that Leonard wouldn't drive right into her gunfire.

Kneeling beside the BMW, Lin called for her dog and when Nicky crawled to her on his stomach, she lifted him into her arms and hurried onto the front lawn where she stood to see Maggie raise her gun and fire over and over at Leonard's windshield.

Leonard wheeled the truck to the side and deliberately crashed it into the sedan sending the car hurtling in Maggie's direction. He leapt from the cab of the truck and rushed towards Lin who had crouched on the grass with her sweet dog cradled in her arms.

"She tried to poison us," Lin yelled. "She poisoned Maura and Warren."

Leonard lifted Lin to her feet, took the dog into his own arms, and was about to hustle them around the side of the palatial home to the tree line away from Maggie when he heard a groan.

"Stay here." Leonard pushed his phone into Lin's hands and jogged to the driveway where he used his truck for cover as he walked around it to get a look at the woman.

Maggie was on her back in front of her vehicle,

unconscious. The gun rested on the crushed-shell driveway. When Leonard's truck crashed into the BMW, the force sent it careening across the driveway where it hit the woman.

"Coffin," Leonard yelled. "We'll be needing an ambulance."

∽

The police and the ambulance arrived. Maggie Topper was taken away to the hospital, alive, but unconscious.

Lin gave her account of what had happened at the Topper house and directed the officers to her cooler at the rear of the home where the dog's bowl and her water bottle were safely tucked inside as evidence that Maggie had attempted to poison them.

Two hours later, the police were still working the scene and Lin, feeling weak and shaky, sat on the front steps of the Topper's house with Nicky on her lap and her head resting on Leonard's shoulder.

"You figured it out, Coffin. And you lived to see another day."

"Thanks to you. If you hadn't come back, she would have killed me."

"Well, she didn't get that chance." Leonard took a

deep breath. "Her killing days are over ... and that is thanks to you."

Lin's phone buzzed with a text from Anton. The police had found her phone inside the house and returned it to her. "Anton says that he's found notes and records that show Vernon Willard bought this land in the spring of 1843. He had this house built in 1844." She looked at her partner. "Elise went missing a few months after Willard bought this land. He owned this parcel when he killed her."

Leonard wore a questioning expression, but before he could ask anything, a detective approached them and thanked them for their reports. "A couple of the officers have found a substance in the house that will prove interesting once it's analyzed. I suspect it might be something highly toxic. You were very lucky," he told Lin with a nod. Looking at the dog on Leonard's lap, the detective added, "So were you, little fella." Walking away, he said, "I'll be in touch."

"How about we get outta here?" Leonard asked his partner. He noticed Lin looking across the yard and at the same time, Nicky yipped a happy bark. "What's up?"

A smile had formed over Lin's face. "It's Elise," she said as her forehead scrunched up. The shimmering ghost floated about a foot above the ground and began moving slowly to the side of the house. Her see-through hand gestured for Lin to come along.

"I think she wants me to follow her." Before the young woman stood up, Nicky had jumped from Leonard's lap and ran to the spirit.

"Come with me." Lin tugged on her partner's arm.

The threesome followed the ghost to the trees at the far end of the grassy, open section of the yard. Elise waited for them and then drifted like smoke into the wooded area as her companions stumbled over vines and underbrush.

"Where is she taking us?" Leonard grumped.

Lin didn't say anything, but she thought she knew where her ghost was leading them.

When she reached a huge boulder standing deep in the woods, Elise stopped and hovered next to it making eye contact with Lin.

The dog woofed and wagged his tail.

"What is it?" Leonard asked. "Why did we stop?"

When Elise gave Lin a nod, her form shimmered with silver light, swirled in a rush, and shot into the air above the treetops and was gone.

"Coffin. Why did we stop?"

As Lin stared at the boulder, Nicky rushed forward and began to dig, his paws moving so fast they blurred against the ground.

Lin held onto Leonard's arm and spoke softly. "I think we just found the spot where Vernon Willard buried Elise's body."

25

Maggie Topper survived the injuries from the BMW hitting her in her own driveway. With her lawyer by her side, she confessed to poisoning her husband as well as Maura Wells. She'd discovered Warren's infidelity by hiring a private detective who reported on Warren's visits to the two women, one in Chicago and one in Boston, who did not know that Warren was married and believed they had an honest relationship with the conniving man. Maggie had flown into a rage when she learned of Warren's activities and now claimed to have been in the throes of mental instability when she committed the crimes.

Maura was poisoned while sitting in a coffee shop doing some reading. When she got up to use the restroom, Maggie slipped into Maura's seat and deposited the poison into the woman's coffee. Warren was easier. Knowing that it took the poison from thirty to forty-five minutes to act, Maggie put it into the coffee her husband was drinking right before he left for the restaurant to meet his friends.

Maggie had the same plans for Sofia Rizzo, but because the young woman had been in Europe on business, she had to wait longer than she'd wanted to. When Sofia arrived on Nantucket to speak with the police, it was a pleasant turn of events for Maggie. She wouldn't need to travel to Boston to carry out her plan and, in fact, had prepared the poison for Sofia on the day Lin noticed Maggie was wearing Elise's necklace and was on her way into town to murder Sofia.

Instead, the poison ended up in Lin's water bottle after Lin asked Maggie about the necklace she was wearing and inquired if she knew Maura Wells and Sofia Rizzo.

The necklace that was stolen from Elise's body would eventually be given to Maura's sister, Bridget, and later, passed to Bridget's daughter since they were the only living relatives of Elise Porter.

Elise's bones were uncovered by investigators who dug next to the boulder in the woods behind the Toppers' house. Elise would find a proper resting place in a cemetery plot right next to that of her descendant, Maura Wells, and both women would be accompanied to Chicago by Maura's loving sister.

The strangeness of Vernon Willard murdering Elise and then two hundred years later, a descendant of Willard murdering Elise's descendant was not lost on Lin and Viv and they had several discussions about the poetic justice of Willard's last descendant spending the rest of her life in prison while Elise's relatives, Bridget and her daughter, would carry on their family genes.

"We'll never really know why Vernon Willard killed Elise," Viv said. "That secret is buried in the long-ago years of history. But at least you found her bones."

"And the murders of Maura and Warren have been solved," Lin said.

"Yesterday, when I was dropping the baked goods off at the inn, Patricia told me that her ghost hasn't been seen in the inn for weeks," Viv told her cousin with a smile. "I bet Elise has crossed over."

"I hope she did," Lin said despite the twinge of sorrow she felt knowing she would never see the ghost again. "I hope she's at peace now."

∾

ON A COOLER DAY at the end of September, Lin and Jeff and Viv and John went on a hike in the Middle Moors along the sandy paths and trails. After being immersed in the sadness of the case, Lin felt the need to spend some time outdoors in the beauty and peacefulness of nature.

The couples brought sandwiches and drinks and, under the brilliant blue sky, they ate their lunches sitting on the ground near a lake surrounded by green and gold vegetation.

"You have a new water bottle," Viv said when she saw her cousin remove the blue and white water container from her backpack.

"Yeah," Lin said with a half-smile. "My old one had some awful kind of residue in it."

"You mean poison?" John asked as he munched on his sandwich. "Probably a good idea that you tossed it."

"Actually, the police took it, but I didn't ask to have it back," Lin kidded.

"I don't know how selling the Topper place is going to go," John said. "A murderer owns the place and her ancestor murdered someone and buried the body on the property. Not exactly positive advertising."

"It might take a special buyer to overlook all that," Jeff guessed.

"The person who will overlook those characteristics of the place will also have to be a very wealthy buyer," John shrugged. "It might be hard to find such a person."

"You'll sell it," Viv encouraged. "Someone will come along who will fall in love with it."

"Or maybe it should be knocked down," Lin frowned. "Nothing good has come out of that place."

"Thanks, Lin. There goes my commission," John said.

After lunch, Viv and John wanted to hike down to some ponds, but Lin had something she wanted to do so told them she and Jeff would catch up to them in a little while.

Lin and her boyfriend hiked about a mile north to Altar Rock and when they reached their destination, they turned in slow circles taking in the views of the trees, low bushes, a pond, and a glimpse of the harbor off in the distance.

Lin let out a sigh and Jeff put his arm around her.

"This case was a tough one. It really highlighted the worst of human nature," she said. "Sometimes it really gets to me. These spirits who are unable to cross over because of what was done to them. What if I couldn't see ghosts? What if I never moved back here? What would happen to the spirits then?"

"But you *can* see ghosts and you *did* move back," Jeff squeezed her shoulders. "Maybe it's all meant to be. We know Lilianna helped ghosts and she lived a long, long, life and right before she passed away, you showed up. Was that only coincidence? I don't think so."

Lin turned to face Jeff and looked into his warm, kind eyes. "Do you think there's always someone here who can help them?"

"I wouldn't be surprised at all. There's something special about this island." Jeff chuckled. "Maybe it puts out a call for help when a ghost-seer is about to leave."

Lin grinned. "And someone answers the call?"

"Could be." Jeff pulled her close and hugged her tight for a minute.

When they separated, Lin opened her backpack and took out a beautiful white rose. "I picked the white color because a white rose symbolizes love, devotion, spirituality, and hope."

Lin walked over to Altar Rock and stood in front of it thinking about Elise.

"I've been feeling sort of low on hope lately," she told Jeff. "Why can't people be good to each other?

Why do people cheat and steal and lie and kill? There's more than enough in the world to go around, to share. Will there be a place after death where all the stupid mistakes we make are forgiven? Where all our hurts fall away? Where people can be kind and good to each other?"

A tear rolled down Lin's cheek as she placed the rose on the rock for Elise. "I hope so," she whispered.

She and Jeff stood side by side for a few minutes and then turned to walk away. They were only a few yards from the rock when the whoosh of cold air swirled around Lin and she stopped and looked back.

Her ghost stood glimmering on the other side of the rock wearing a long white dress with a blue ribbon around the waist. Elise's hair was soft and gently fell around her shoulders, and her bright blue eyes held Lin's.

The ghost smiled with such warmth that it filled Lin's heart.

"She's here," she told Jeff in a whispered voice. "I've never seen her look so peaceful ... so light ... so happy."

With a lovely smile on her face, Elise's atoms sparkled silver and gold and began to spin. The ghost put her hand on her heart and bowed her head to Lin, and then the atoms flared into a wild whoosh of white sparkles that shot high into the air like a firework, and were gone.

Lin blinked at the sky for a few moments. "She left," she told Jeff as she reached for him and took his hand in hers.

Jeff said, "You know those questions you just asked, about will our hurts fall away and will there be a place where people will be good to each other? I think Elise just answered them for you."

Lin wrapped her boyfriend in a tight, loving embrace as hope trickled slowly, but surely back into her heart.

THANK YOU FOR READING!

Books by J.A. WHITING can be found here:
www.amazon.com/author/jawhiting

To hear about new books and book sales, please sign
up for my mailing list at:
www.jawhitingbooks.com

Your email will never be sold, shared, or spammed.

If you enjoyed the book, please consider leaving a
review. A few words are all that's needed. It would be
very much appreciated.

BOOKS/SERIES BY J. A. WHITING

CLAIRE ROLLINS COZY MYSTERIES

LIN COFFIN COZY MYSTERIES

PAXTON PARK COZY MYSTERIES

SWEET COVE COZY MYSTERIES

OLIVIA MILLER MYSTERIES (not cozy)

ABOUT THE AUTHOR

J.A. Whiting lives with her family in Massachusetts. Whiting loves reading and writing mystery and suspense stories.

Visit / follow me at:

www.jawhitingbooks.com
www.bookbub.com/authors/j-a-whiting
www.amazon.com/author/jawhiting
www.facebook.com/jawhitingauthor

Made in the USA
Middletown, DE
17 August 2018